TOM COLLINS

Tom Collins

A **SLIGHTLY CROOKED** NOVEL

DOUGLAS VIGLIOTTI

TOM COLLINS: A 'Slightly Crooked' Novel
by Douglas Vigliotti

Published by Slightly Crooked

www.slightlycrooked.pub

Copyright © 2021 Douglas Vigliotti. All rights reserved. No portion of this book may be reproduced in any form without permission from the publisher, except as permitted by U.S. copyright law. For permissions contact the publisher.

Disclaimer: This is a work of fiction. Names, characters, business, events and incidents are the products of the author's imagination. Any resemblance to actual persons, living or dead, or actual events is purely coincidental.

ISBN: 978-1-7375482-0-1 (paperback)

Printed in U.S.A.

First Edition

Visit the authors website at: www.douglasvigliotti.com.

To Lia, Joey, James, Nick, & Chris, I hope you create something special one day.

> *Anything you absorb you will ultimately secrete. It's inevitable. Most of us are original paintings, and it's a mystery as to what is learned and what is borrowed, what is stolen and what is born, what you came in with and what you found while you were here.*

— TOM WAITS

ONE

THE ROOM IS HOLLOW. My couch feels like hardened clay and the walls are closing in on me. The TV is playing a sad love song, and the upper right corner reads 5.51am. How did I get here?

Not physically, I can retrace my steps, but mentally is more my concern. I should be careful what I ask for, unpacking that might do more harm than good. When you've been up for 24 hours straight, your brain starts to feel like it's glued together with epoxy, synapses stop firing, and you become an emotional wrecking ball. Destroying every good feeling inside your heart. You're left with a pile of ashes to do your thinking for you.

Typically, I'd be drinking coffee right now, but I'm operating in reverse. There's light creeping through the edge of the closed blinds and I can only dream of sleeping. I wish the afterparty never stopped. The living room that once felt like Studio 54 has now turned into a cold park bench. I'm a bum inside my own home—weak, hungry, and yearning for another warm body.

Last night got a little out of hand. It started off as a

casual Friday evening. I downed my first Tom Collins around 7pm and continued to pour them down my throat for the next five hours. Most people call that alcoholism and by the book they're probably right. If that's the case, then almost everyone I know is an alcoholic. What am I supposed to do? Be the only one not drinking? Only recovering addicts and stiffs don't drink. That's what everyone is thinking. True or not, does it matter? Plus, the days are too long to not drink on the weekends.

I take the train into Manhattan every day and Metro-North is a disaster. Where do I start? It hasn't been updated in at least 30 years. It's slow. It's crowded. It smells like a dirty sock. But some people love taking the train. Time to think or something. Me? I can't stand it. It's a daily reminder of the slog—a shitty feeling. You meet some decent people, but I've never seen more people dressed up with nowhere to go. All of them, in a rush, feeling more important than they are, and ready to tell you about it. I mean, they're going somewhere but, honestly, where? Work?

They're just wearing costumes until they get the chance to be who they really are. Every day is Halloween.

All I wanted to do when I grew up was to wear one of those costumes. Wall Street type or some business executive. That was my dream. Tight suits, straight ties, and shiny shoes. Never made it to Wall Street exactly, but I got the costume. I work for Perkins LP selling financial data. We're global, but our headquarters are based in the city. I'm basically a number in a sea of numbers, but hey—the benefits are good. That's the lure, the bait. It was all I needed as an impressionable young kid after I graduated from the University of Rhode Island. For better or worse, they were right. Seven years later, I earn a six-figure salary, drive a BMW, and rent a $2,500-per-month apartment in

Stamford, CT. I guess I got what I always wanted. The American dream. I just need a wife, two kids, and a mortgage. So why do I hate myself for it?

And just like that we're back to the alcohol. That end-of-the-week drink sounds tempting once you realize things aren't what you imagined them to be. It's not so much the drink on a Friday night that's bad, though. It's the after-midnight session where things can take a turn for the worse. Last night was one of those nights. I ran into Luke Handley. Him and I go way back. It's part of the deal, living where we grew up. Just like they said in *Cheers*, everybody knows your name, even the Devil. Handley isn't a bad guy, per se, but he escalates the night. He's reckless. He provides mental stimulation, wanted or unwanted, and then his name is suddenly spelled out on the coffee table in coke dust. Fuckin' Handley.

Is that a knock on the door?

There's only one thing that makes your skin crawl more than a 24-hour bender. A knock on your door right at the precipice, the point when angst is so high that a knock might as well be a gunshot. The combination of weakness and possibility is just too much to bear. The thought that a sober person might be on the other side of the door will scare even the toughest bastards.

A spider creeps up my neck, perches on my head, and tickles my conscience. Who the hell could this be? Am I hallucinating? It's an apartment building. Nobody comes here unintentionally, especially not at six in the morning on a Saturday. That spider starts to crawl down my spine, sending a strange tingling sensation to all of my extremities.

Shit. It's definitely a knock. Two or three more follow.

Should I just sit here and hope they go away? I could use a friend right now. Ugh, I pry myself limb after limb from the couch, grab my Louisville Slugger, and head to the door.

I look through the peephole and there's two women standing there. One looks like she just got out from underneath a jackhammer and the other is tall and gangly. What the hell?

I open the door and ask, "Can I help you?"

"We're here for . . . you know," the tall one says.

"No, I don't know," I say. "What are you doing here?"

"We were texting a guy named Luke and he gave this address. You know, we're here to have some fun."

"Fun?" I ask.

"Uh, yeah. We came all the way from Rhode Island."

Is it possible I know these chicks? Nah, unless I'm delusional there's no way. Of course, that's also possible. "Rhode Island!? That's a long way," I blurt out. "How do you know Luke?"

They look at each other, confused. The same woman responds, "We don't. I just met him tonight. He messaged us."

Messaged us? I finally put two and two together. These women are prostitutes.

Damn it, Handley. This is what I mean. Not a bad guy, but shit—what the hell? The sun is coming up, I'm teetering on insanity, and now there are two pros standing in my doorway. Who orders sex and forgets about it? Or just leaves? It's asinine. I like fun, but street girls? I should send them packing, but they did drive all the way from Rhode Island.

"Come inside, come inside," I say. "Do I need to pay you or something?"

"$200 each," the tall one says.

"$200 each!? I didn't even order you."

"That's not my problem."

"What about $100 flat?"

"You're crazy," she says. "It's not going to work. Gas alone was $40, and we skipped another job to get here."

I rub my eyes, run my hands through my hair, Handley really did it to me this time. Should I tell them to go screw and head back to Rhode Island? Is this a bad dream?

Damn, that bleeding heart again. I gotta pay. Maybe I should just get a blow job? I mean, I'm paying anyway. This is terrible.

"Fine, whatever. I'll pay you $400," I say. "Look, I'm not even going to sleep with you. Let's just burn one down, shoot the shit for a while, then you can head back. Do you at least have some weed?"

"Really? That's all you want?" she asks.

"That's all," I reply. The silent one looks at the tall one doing all the talking and they both look perplexed by the situation. The silent one throws her arms up in the air.

The tall one shrugs, then says, "Well, I guess there's a first time for everything."

As soon as she puts her hand out, I remember something. "Sorry, I got a minor problem. I don't have any cash on me."

"Are you joking?"

"I'm not, but I can PayPal you."

"PayPal!?" she barks.

"What do you want me to tell you?" I snap back. "I have no other way. I've been up since 5am yesterday, worked all day, partied all night, then you two show up like Batman and Robin looking to save the day."

"Fine, whatever," she says.

It does get me thinking, though. How much sex money even goes through PayPal? Millions? Picture that slogan. PayPal, your trusted provider of illegal activity and conduit of fun to ensure your party never ends. What a joke.

We make the digital transaction, pour a few drinks, and twist up a joint.

You haven't lived until you've hung out with the underworld. It's more real than those costumes on the train, that's for sure. There's no hiding anything. Who am I kidding? Half of those costumes are probably living some more bizarre shit than this.

Here's how I see it. You can break people up into three groups. The pre-midnight crowd, which is your average stiff. Saddled by their spouse, kids, and American idealism, easy to peg and rather uninteresting. Then, there's the after-midnight crowd which is pretty interesting. They're the people who can talk about the dark side, but not really go there, maybe they danced with it in college. But they still know how to have some fun. Then there's the after-4am crowd that really opens your eyes to the world. You want empathy for people? Smoke a joint with two hookers who drove over two hours at 4.30 in the morning just to earn a living. Say what you want about morality, but that's as real as it gets. All of a sudden, 9-to-5 doesn't seem so bad. Neither does the grumpy neighbor or that a-hole cousin. Plus, it's quite liberating. You can say whatever you want. It's all on the table. There's nothing you can say that's going to offend the underworld. What can be more extreme than the reality these two girls live?

With a head full of marijuana, inhibitions start to drift away, and we talk about all kinds of stuff. Stories about the rotten scum we've encountered. The corporate world and the underworld. Turns out rotten is rotten. You'd be amazed at the similarities. They even let me moan about work. Something about not being appreciated for the amount I do. Sucks to admit, but I love recognition.

"I hear you," the tall one says. "Most times we don't even get a thank you."

Imagine that? How brutal. She gets it, though. I'm actually having a good time. And for a moment, that cold park bench turns into a warm sofa again.

"Do you play?" the tall one asks. "Or does that thing just collect dust?"

"Play what?"

She points to the corner of the room. I turn my head.

"Oh, the guitar," I say. "Well, I don't see any dust on it."

"Funny," she says. "So are you like a musician or something?"

"I wouldn't go that far. Music has always just been a refuge; a chance to escape into a song and lose my identity. I'm enamored with the fortitude of a musician; it's always struck me as a commitment to zig when others zagged. Tough road. Real backbone. In another life, maybe I would have been one."

They egg me on to play a tune. 'Here Comes the Sun' seems appropriate, so I give it a go. They laugh and I smile. I screw up a good two or three times. Totally immersed, they don't catch it. Most people are impressed with such a base level of skill. Let alone spot a few technical flubs. Maybe it's the cannabis that has them spinning. It has me spinning. Probably a blend of both. Either way, it always feels good to hear them say, "Wow. That was really good."

"Do another," the tall one says.

I rest the guitar down and take a swig of my drink.

Before I can pick the guitar back up, the silent one finally speaks, "How do you not have a girlfriend? You seem like you have your shit together."

Only a street worker would have the balls to suggest this in the wee hours of the morning. I'm over here walking on water and she finds me endearing. Seems questionable at best.

"You want the truth?" I say.

They both nod.

"Here it is," I say. "Romantic relationships can be great, but I know the reality of what happens as they age. They *always* require work. So, the real question is . . . How bad do you want to fight for the relationship? Seems shitty to even have to think about, but it's the truth. I've never envisioned myself actually being able to fight for someone." I stop for a moment, take a sip of gin, and ponder. They just sit there staring at me like they see a ghost.

"You know, I guess it's like The Beatles once sang in 'Something'," I say. "That something is hard to pinpoint, but either way that question always looms: Will I want to fight for you?"

"I have a question, though," the silent one says.

"Shoot."

"If you never met that person, how do you know if you want to fight for them?"

It's kind of disappointing to even hear that response. I expected a more honest understanding from the underworld. These people have been punched in the face by reality enough times to know when they hear the truth. The question has me thinking that these two sex workers might want to take me to the bedroom. Are they getting an emotional attachment or something? I have to erase that idea with my next response.

"Obviously, I gotta want to fuck her. You know, be physically attracted to her," I say. "But that's the thing about physical attraction, it grows when there are other elements that pull you in. Maybe it's the way she dresses. Possibly an elegance. Perhaps an edginess. Or even wittiness or intelligence. They're all magnifiers of attraction.

It's that *something* the Beatles were talking about. I can't pinpoint it, but I need it. Otherwise I'll never fight for you."

I notice my gin is nearing the bottom, so I lean forward, grab the glass, and gulp it down in one clean swipe. As the empty glass hits the coffee table I say, "I guess I gotta want to fuck you, then want to fight for you."

The girls start to laugh, and I can't help but chuckle myself.

"Look, when two people spend a lot of time together, it's inevitable, they will start to annoy the shit out of each other. It's just the reality of the situation. It's human nature. No matter what, that day will come when you have to fight."

I lean back on the sofa, let off a sigh, and they're speechless.

Imagine saying that on an actual date. The person across from you will think you're psychotic, but, honestly, I don't know if I can explain it any better. I'd probably just say something stupid or worse, what I think she wants to hear me say to her. Doomed from the start, how can you recover? You don't. You wear that costume until one day it gets ripped off and your own girlfriend is looking at you like you're a monster.

Meanwhile you're just sitting there, looking back, and saying, "What? This is who I am. Christian. Christian Ballantine."

I run my hand through my hair, then look over at the clock. It reads 8am. Thank God today is Saturday.

"Alright girls, it's been real, but I gotta get some shuteye."

"Yeah, we should probably head back," the tall one says. "I'm so happy to have met you."

"And thanks," the silent one says.

"Thanks for what?"

"For talking with us," she says. The tall one chimes in, "Yeah, you're a good guy." I guess I'll take it where I could get it.

We hug, they leave, and finally, I can sleep.

TWO

I LIMP OUT of the bedroom, wipe the eye boogers off, and, surprisingly, my body doesn't feel terrible. It's my mind that's warped like a piece of wet wood. I slam down 600mg of Ibuprofen hoping that'll do the trick. The living room is still a warzone from last night. Christ, maybe I should take an extra 200mg. I do, then grab my phone.

It's 5pm? Damn, I wasted an entire Saturday. I guess that's what I get for being a savage last night.

Nobody calls anymore. It's always text messages and I have three from Jack Young. He's one of my closest buddies. Also, he happens to be single. That's the thing when you get to your 30s. You have fewer and fewer friends who are single. Something like a domino effect, once one starts the marriage train, it's just one after the other. They start dropping like flies in their late 20s. Before then, even if they're dating someone they still go out with their single friends, but you don't start to feel isolated until 30. Now, all of a sudden, you went from an acceptable friend to hang out with to a dangerous one. Your friends need to start making excuses to hang out with you. Maybe even lie a little bit. God forbid the married guy hangs out with the single guy. I get it. Two different agendas. I guess whatever makes your other half sleep well at night.

Jack is 33, married young, but divorced about two years ago. He kind of looks like a Ken doll—dusty blonde hair, light eyes, and square chin. Maybe he belongs on a beach in California. His ex was a sweetheart, but he couldn't keep his dick in his pants. He's an asshole, but, like Keith Richards said, "Most guys I know are assholes, I have some great asshole friends, but that's not the point. Friendship has got nothing to do with that. It's can you hang, can you talk about this without any feeling of distance between you?" So yeah, that's our relationship. I never understood how he got married in the first place. Some guys just shouldn't get married, he's one of those guys, addicted to the rush. His text messages read:

(9.07am) Jack: "Breakfast at 10?"

(11.12am) Jack: "Call me when you get up."

(3.22pm) Jack: "Damn, you musta had a rough one."

I consider my response for a minute. Does it even matter? The conversation will end with him getting me to go out again tonight. That thought alone makes the hair on the back of my neck stand up. But it is only Saturday. As long as tonight doesn't turn into a circus, I can get to bed at a normal hour, 1 or 2am. Wake up at 7 or 8am, relax on Sunday, then business as usual on Monday. Good enough for me, so I text him.

Me: "Oh man I got a story for you."

Jack: "Lol, good one?"

Me: "Crazy one. I'll tell you when I see ya."

Jack: "Christ must be bad. What's good for tonight???"

Me: "NO city. Last night was rough. Fatty Duck?"

Jack: "It's all old chicks."

Me: "Lol, great oysters tho."

Jack: "True, whatever. Grab res for 830."
Me: "Meet at your house?"
Jack: "Yup."
Me: "See ya soon."

I'm not big on texting but it gets the job done. Short and sweet. At least you don't have to sit there on the phone hemming and hawing. "Uh, I don't know. What do you want to do?" Those convos are the worst. I'd rather stick a pen in my ear and fall sideways. Or go out for round two after a 24-hour bender.

Jack's house is gorgeous. Not massive, more like a villa. Brick, stucco, Spanish tile roof. Good size yard. Doesn't look like it belongs in Connecticut, but he built it from the ground up. That's his business, though. He's a residential builder. Actually, it's the family business. Jack is an only child, his Dad, who is very old, doesn't do much anymore, so Jack basically runs the business. Good money, much different from the corporate racket I'm caught up in. Couple big stings and they set you up for a while, whereas my work is more of a daily grind with a steady stream of income. His ex-wife could have taken the house, but she didn't want anything to do with it after she found some girl in their bed. Most women would have taken their husband to the cleaners. I don't know if that says more about her or Jack. I mean, despite the situation, he had her under some kind of spell.

Long story short: Jack got to keep the house. It sits in a little area of Norwalk called Rowayton. Near the Long Island Sound. He keeps saying, "I'm going to sell this damn thing." He's been saying that since the divorce settled about 18 months ago. I'll believe it when I see it.

The villa is like a skeleton house. No blood, no warmth. You can tell a woman hasn't lived there in almost two years. It's not that he has bad taste, but all the love is gone. No food in the fridge, just vodka and cranberry juice, and a couple blocks of extra-sharp cheddar cheese. I don't mind, though. Except that he never has gin, never mind club soda or lemon juice. Selfish bastard.

I walk through the door and yell out, "Yoooo!" I hear some stomping on the ceiling above.

Jack yells, "Be right down! Just finishing up getting ready!"

We always congregate in the kitchen, so I head over to one of the high tops next to the kitchen island. I look around, check my phone a few times, nothing seems out of place. Then hear: boom, boom, boom. Footsteps coming downstairs. With a big smile on his face, Jack shouts, "Ohhh! You're alive."

I laugh. "Yeah. I'm alive alright."

"So, what the hell happened last night?" he asks.

"You're *never* going to believe this shit."

I tell him the story and he's practically hysterical. He gathers himself, then says, "Wait—two pros showed up at 6am. And you didn't even get a blowjob? What the . . .but you smoked a joint, played the guitar, and bullshitted for two hours?"

It does sound pretty ridiculous. Honestly, I don't really want to talk about it. Shit, I just lived it. That's bad enough, even if the company ended up being better than most. I tend to put things behind me and move forward. Once something happens, good or bad, it's over, onward and upward.

Of course, he wants details. People love seeing your failures and hearing about your imperfections. Successes and strengths, not so much. It's something you learn from being in sales for years. Failures make people feel good about their own fuckups. It's like, "Ah, we're all on this path together." Successes just leave people saying, "What makes him so special?" Or, "I wish the world knew what he was really like." Yes, even your friends. They're probably the worst. Remember: assholes.

Personally, last night's bullshit doesn't bother me too much. It didn't violate a principle I sort of live by: you can do bad shit to yourself, but don't do bad shit to other people. This doesn't work for everybody, but I can handle it. It's not that I want to, but at least I know I'm not hurting anybody else. I've danced with the after-4am crowd too many times. There's a lot of walking wounded after 4am. Social outlaws that have been unjustly hurt too often in life. A disturbing sight at times, even for a cowboy. Hurt yourself, but never anybody else. Another lesson in empathy from the underworld.

I don't pay attention to Jack's ball busting. My ears only open when I hear the word, "Ready?"

I look at my watch. "Let's rock 'n' roll."

He walks to the fridge, opens the door, and looks over his shoulder.

"Road soda?"

"Let's just go. The place is 10 minutes away," I say. "And we're only going to dinner, dude."

THREE

FATTY DUCK is busy tonight. It's a small place with two sections: a dining area and a big U-shaped bar. A wall on the open end of the U-bar divides the two sections. The dining area has about a dozen tables. It's got a fireplace and hardwood decorating the entire interior—walls, ceiling, and floor. It almost feels like a log cabin in Vermont. You can smell the smoke, taste the maple syrup, and feel the heat from the fire.

Every time Jack and I go to eat, it's an unspoken race for the better seat. Inevitably there's always one seat that's better than the other. Usually, it's the one that faces people. Tonight, I get the good one. Perfect to survey the crowd. Jack has to look at my yapping mug and the wall behind me. Sorry, bud.

We usually talk about the same shit over and over. Mostly work and women. What else do two single guys talk about? Tonight's conversation is no different. Jack kicks it off with the usual, "How's work going?" This sets me off on a tangent, one that feels eerily similar to the rant I gave those pros last night.

"I'm actually killing it," I say. "But I feel like I'm not getting the recognition I deserve."

"What does recognition matter? You're making money, right?"

He brings up a good point, but that's not how it works in the corporate world. The recognition is half the game.

"It's true. I am," I say. "But here's the thing. When push comes to shove, the only thing that matters is what the big guys think of you. You're never safe. A restructuring, some sticky situation, maybe a merger, a new guy steps in and—boom—just like that your job is gone. All you're left with is a résumé. Awards, recognition, they're important. They show how you stack up to everyone else. Right or wrong. It matters."

Jack smirks and says, "So you're telling me you're worried about something that might never happen?"

"Oh, it happens," I say. "And when it does you don't even see it coming. It hits like a gut shot. You're left breathless."

"Gut shot," he says, still smirking. "You're too much." He thinks my lingo is funny, but it's reality. The essence of all good humor is the truth.

"Well, next weekend is the year-end awards dinner," I say. "I'm in the running for the Rising Star Award. It's a big deal in the company. Last year, I lost out on it to some jackass who isn't even with the company anymore. It was a joke. His selling territory was from Midtown to Battery Park. You can't walk two feet without bumping into a financial company. You'd have a tougher time scoring in a whore house."

He just looks at me. "Rising Star Award? I don't know, dude. Sounds like some bullshit to me."

I look up. There's a fine crack in the ceiling paint. I

follow it across the room. It reminds me of all the little things in life that go unnoticed.

"Maybe you're right," I say. "You know, not everything that matters can be quantified—I just wish they'd fuckin' realize that."

Jack's not even paying attention. He's ordering our drinks from the waiter. "Vodka soda for me and a Tom Collins for him." He turns to me and raises his voice, "Look, forget about it for now. Let's just enjoy the night."

Ah, maybe he was listening. What the hell. We order a dozen east coast oysters, couple filet mignons, and a side of creamed spinach to split. Far cry from last night's debacle. Life ain't so bad, I guess.

We're sitting in the nearside corner, wall to my right and backside, and facing the bar area. The only thing that separates my left side from the fireplace is another four-top. Two older, married couples. All drinking red wine. The fellas look like attorney types, tight haircuts, clean shaven, and button-down shirts with the sleeves cuffed. Their wives look to be having a good time, hair down, and smiles from cheek to cheek. Each with a designer bag hanging over her chair.

Directly behind Jack, there's another two-seater with two guys wearing costumes, no not real costumes—suits. They must be doing "business." Diagonal from us, right over Jack's left shoulder is another four-top. Only two ladies, though. Now, these two look like they're just having a casual night out. Similar to Jack and I, just older. Not by much. Maybe late-30s to early-40s. The one facing me has long brown hair, big fancy eyeglasses, dark frames, and a tall glass of white wine in front of her. She looks well put together. The other woman's face is hidden. She's sitting in an open-back chair looking the other direction. She has perfectly edged shoulders coming out of a black sleeveless turtleneck sweater, waist-high jeans, and dirty blonde hair tied up in a bun. I can see the edge of a martini glass. Blowing off steam? She looks like it.

As the night wanes on, Jack eventually goes to take a leak, and I feel a wave of fatigue hit me like a sack of potatoes. I'm sitting here dazed, mushy, and feeling the effects of last night's debauchery. Should I call it a night? Nah, Jack wouldn't have it. Dinner is just the shotgun start; things typically find their pace after the meal. The bar is starting to fill in. Jack comes back from the bathroom. "Grab a drink at the bar?" I suggest.

"Did the bill come?" he asks. Just as the words fall out of his mouth, the bill arrives, we chop it two ways, and head to the bar.

Whoa—I haven't stood up for at least an hour. It's interesting, people have told me when they stand up they feel drunker. I'm sort of the opposite, that uh-oh-I-might-be-getting-drunk feeling happens when I'm sitting in the same spot for too long. It fades within minutes once I get on my feet. I'd rather be like a spinning top. It distracts me.

I'm only a couple cocktails deep, but there's a glaze spread over my eyes. I've learned to love the glaze. It's the sweet spot, eyes that are perfectly gin-dipped, and it's happening at the right time. It's a little after 11pm and the dining area is all but cleared out. I look over toward the bar and it's packed. All that remains are people flirting, chatting, and throwing them back. Oh, and the DJ finally starts to play a few tunes.

I spot an opening at the corner of the bar. Shimmying my way through the crowd, I glance at Jack. "What do you want?"

He shouts, "Vodka with a splash of water."

This could be an annoying wait, there's only one bartender. Do I become the annoying guy and start waving my hand? Of course I do, and it gets her attention. I pull my hand back. Wham—my elbow hits a glass behind me, and I hear a gasp.

"You've got to be kidding me," a voice says. I twist my head around. It's the perfectly-edged-shouldered woman. The one with her back to me at dinner.

I shout above the noise of the music, "I'm so sorry!"

Her friend is laughing, which makes me crack a smile, but the perfectly-edged-shoulder woman is looking down at vodka splattered all over her snug blue jeans. She flips her head up and looks me right in the eye, "You think this is funny!?"

Holy shit. Her green eyes seem to burn a hole right through me. I feel a tingle go through my body that awakens my mouth. "No, I'm so sorry. It was just . . . your friend was . . . "

"Save it," she says, "It's okay, we're just about to leave."

Her friend butts in, "We were?"

"Yes. We were."

Her friend seems to be having fun with this. "I don't remember that," she says, then laughs.

Is this serendipity? If so, I'll have to recover. There's no way I'm letting this woman leave. It's like someone carved her out of stone and embedded emeralds in her head for eyes. I have to think of something quick.

"Don't let me ruin the night. Let me buy you another drink," I say. "It's the least I can do."

The friend nudges her. "Yeah Liv. Let him buy you a drink."

The friend is clearly being facetious, but it gets me excited. Am I "Liv's" type or something? It was an insinuation that might suggest, "What, are you dumb or something? Of course let him buy you a drink." Maybe that's just how I heard it. Shit, I hope not. Either way, I'm going for it.

"Liv, is it?"

"Yes," she says.

"What are you drinking?"

"Vodka martini, shaken not stirred, three olives," she says.

"Watch James Bond much?"

She tilts her head and squints her eyes. "What?"

"Nothing, he drinks those," I say.

"Ohhh." Shit, I guess that one didn't land.

I turn back around to order the drinks; the bartender is gone. Has it really been that long? Damn it, I have to be that asshole and do the flag down move again. Whatever Liv is worth it.

Now I see Jack in the corner of my eye, flagging me down, and pointing at his watch. He picks up his phone, points to it, then points at me. I have a text from him, "Let's go to a new spot. This place is filled with cougars."

No way I'm leaving now. Jack and I haven't even had a drink yet and I got a cross between Charlize Theron and Kate Beckinsale waiting for me to order her one. I text him back, "Come here. Just ordered your drink."

The Rolling Stones song 'Miss You' is playing in the background. You can't mistake that sax solo, it's a lightning bolt straight to the heart. It makes your blood flow. Perfect timing, really. I'm feeling it. I spin back around with drinks in hand. There's a sea of people and everything looks out of focus, except Liv. Is she glowing? Not possible, maybe it's a sign she's got a hold on me.

Liv thanks me as I hand her the martini. Feeling good, I took the liberty to buy her friend one as well.

"Oh no," says the friend. "I don't drink martinis."

I laugh and ask, "Why, will something bad happen?"

She shakes her head as if to say fine and she grabs it out of my hand.

Jack comes strutting around the corner. "Where's my drink?" I hold it up in the air and he snatches it out of my hand.

I lean over to his left ear. "I met two ladies. Let me introduce you. Blondie is mine."

He smiles and says, "Oh yeah?"

I raise my voice, "Jack, these are my two new friends, Liv and . . . sorry, I didn't even get your name."

She shouts over the music, "Emma." Jack shakes each of their hands and introduces himself. Liv taps my shoulder.

"Alright, mystery man," she says. "The only person's name we don't know is yours."

I look straight at her. "My name is Christian. Do you want me to spell it for you?"

"Oh so you're a wise guy, too."

"Only when I'm intrigued," I say.

She laughs. "Oh, you're intrigued, are you? How old are you anyway?"

"I'm 30."

We stand there looking at each other for a minute, then Liv breaks the silence.

"It's okay. You can ask how old I am."

Honestly, I don't give a shit, but I play the game. When she says 41, it doesn't surprise me. Either way, I have eyes for her.

She shouts, "I bet you can't tell me who's playing right now?"

Like I don't know it's the Rolling Stones. Her eyes open up when I tell her. A jab at my age? Blocked.

"Tell me something I wouldn't know by looking at you," she says. I tell her I play the guitar. She just grins, takes a sip of her drink, her eyes never losing contact with mine. "So, would you play me a song?"

Such a typical comment. I smile from ear to ear though. "Maybe one day."

"You don't really play guitar," she says. "Do you?"

I laugh and say, "And that's not Mick Jagger singing right now."

She looks at me, confused. Damn it. My jokes aren't landing.

"Yes, I play the guitar," I say earnestly. We both smile.

"Very cool," she says. "My Dad used to play the guitar. Music was a big part of my childhood."

"What was playing in the house?" I ask.

"Oh, classics—Beatles, Dylan, Petty, Beach Boys, and all those Laurel Canyon artists."

She knows rock 'n' roll, and we chat about it for the next 20 minutes. There are a few guys at work who could hold their own, but on the whole I was starving for this conversation. Let alone with a woman that looks like her.

The night is rolling on and I think Liv is on martini number three or four. I'm not really counting. Jack is starting to get restless, something fell through with Emma, and now he's nagging me to leave. I tell him, "No way I'm fuckin' leaving." He looks disappointed, but what am I going to do?

I want this woman and it feels like she wants me. There's no better feeling in the world. I ask Jack, "Do you care if I stay here with her?"

He shakes his head. "Do what you gotta do, man." I throw my hands up to each side and shrug my shoulders.

He knows that I ain't budging and he's dying for more action. "Alright! Make it worth it. I'm outta here," he says. "I'll catch up with you mañana."

Believe it or not, this might actually screw me. Emma

could insist that they should leave. But what happens next is actually a small gift from God. Emma runs into some guy she knows. He has to be 50-something. He looks like a washed-up rock star. Distressed leather jacket, beaded bracelets up and down both wrists, long messy hair, couple rips in his tight jeans, and black boots. There's no more than a foot or two separating their faces. And when they look our way their smiles suggest they're at ease with each other. Old fling? Maybe. No time to analyze further, all I know is this probably means more time with Liv.

Liv's smile is infectious. It isn't perfect, but it is damn near close. Just a faint gap between her two snow-white front teeth. Almost like she had it done that way on purpose. Did she?

There are two things that are dead giveaways that a woman likes you: laughing and touching. There are copious amounts of both happening. Now all I can think about is slipping my hand around her waist, lifting up that tight black turtleneck sweater, and grabbing the small of her back to bring her close to me. I'm growing just thinking about it.

The first time she puts her hair down I almost blow straight out of my boots. Holy bejeezus, I think. It's then I realize just what kind of fox I have in front of me. We stay away from any conversation that might ruin the moment. Don't ask, don't tell. The only time we get close is when I voluntarily tell her I am single. She just looks at me and tilts her head. "I don't believe that," she says. "How do you not have a girlfriend?"

Deep down I want to think of something clever, but I can only remember my answer to the same question last night with the prostitutes. "Because I haven't found anyone I want to fight for yet," I blurt out.

"Fight for?" She says.

This sets me off on my spiel about always having to fight for the girl. The same one I gave the girls last night. "If you can't see yourself fighting for her, then why ever make them your girlfriend or wife. You always gotta fight for the relationship."

"*But* how do you know if you don't give them a chance?"

Am I really going to answer this the same way? Screw it, why not? So I look her dead in the eye and say, "You've got to want to fuck her first. Not: 'Ah okay, I'll sleep with that person.' I mean, you really want to fuck her. It *has* to start that way."

Liv shakes her head, opens her eyes, and laughs. Her facial expression suggests she's struck by my bluntness, but the shock on her face starts to fade. Now those green eyes are giving me that look. Everyone knows that look.

I don't realize until this moment, but my hand has been cupping the small of her back. The same way I was daydreaming about just 30 minutes ago. I resist the urge to ask any relationship questions. She isn't wearing a ring, that's good enough for me, so I just let her continue to pry on me. My watch reads 12.30am, so I think it is time to drop the bomb: "Do you want to go back to my place?"

She looks at me, looks around for Emma, and she is nowhere to be found. Probably ran off with John Varvatos or something. I can tell she wants to say yes, but there is a slight hesitancy. She bites her lip, thinks about it for a moment. "Let's go."

I evaporate into a million tiny pieces of confetti that sprinkle over us to celebrate the occasion. Champagne is popping and horns are blowing. What a moment. Then I snap back to reality and say, "Okay, I'll grab the Uber."

The ride back to my apartment is only ten minutes, but it feels like an hour. I can't wait to get there soon enough.

Liv's head is in the phone, out of the phone, in the phone, out of the phone. What is she doing? Is she worried? Each time I look at her, I'm nervous she might drop the axe on the whole thing. Caput, I gotta go home. The Uber driver shouts back, "Sorry I missed the turn." What the fuck? Is this guy trying to torture me?

I briefly think about the scene in my apartment last night. Imagine if Liv knew that. What would she think? It doesn't matter because she'll never know. Unless there's some remnants lingering around the apartment. Are there remnants lingering around? I didn't exactly spot clean the place prior to leaving for Jack's earlier. Shit, I hope it's not disgusting. Fuck. I'm too tipsy at this point to even care.

The confetti starts to fall again. Liv's hand touches my left leg, and it is slowly making its way over to an over-grown bulge in my tight jeans. Before I know it, her well-manicured hands have a fistful. We haven't even kissed yet. I look over to my left; she is looking dead at me, but her dirty blonde hair covers her right eye. The other one has more than enough napalm to set me on fire. Maybe even melt me. I can feel the heat rise from between my legs. I think about leaning in right there, but the build-up is starting to get too intense. Why ruin it? We're about to be two uncaged animals at any moment. The tension breaks when we hear the driver say, "Here."

There's another hidden benefit to an Uber—it's not a moment-killer. It's a thank you and you're out the door. The tension begins to mount again. We hold hands, stride by the doorman and lobby attendant, and hit the elevator button. I can see her eyes go from light to dark green. From excitement to lust. From want to need. I can see the freak inside getting ready to crawl out.

The elevator door opens, we hop inside, and I hit the close button with my left index finger three times. Her grip on my right hand gets tighter and tighter. As soon as the double doors slide shut, there isn't even a second wasted, she pushes me against the wall, throws her knee between my legs, grabs the back of my head, and pulls me in close. I return the favor, grab her by the waist and pull her the rest of the way in. Our lips interlock like two puzzle pieces that have long been missing from each other. They never lose contact, moving in complete harmony. I'm certain she can feel me throbbing. Everything is magnified as her grasp on the back of my head gets stronger and stronger. Just as the tension is reaching its peak, the elevator doors slide open.

We stumble down the hall, I grab her ass, and she swats my hand in a playful way. Flipping that dirty blonde hair back, now looking over her shoulder at me with a devilish smile, permanently branded in my mind.

I fumble the key as I try to unlock the door. She laughs, then says, "What, are you nervous or something?"

The key slides into the keyhole. I look back, snag her with my right arm, push the door open with my left shoulder. We both fall into my apartment, Liv lying on top of me, and we hear the door slam shut behind us.

I brush her hair to the side, look her in the eyes, and say, "Nervous? Not at all."

We share a laugh and it is our last. The rest of the night is spent howling like two wolves while confetti pours down from the moon.

FOUR

Sᴜɴᴅᴀʏ ᴍᴏʀɴɪɴɢ is a little different from Saturday. Birds are chirping and 'Miss You' is playing over and over in my head. Nobody wakes up pretty, actually, most people resemble a monster crawling out of their hole. Great sex makes you feel angelic, wakes up your soul, and even makes morning breath smell like daisies. It just does something to you. That's the running joke at work, right? You know, when someone is more pleasant than normal. Ah, they *must* have gotten laid last night. Now I know the genesis. I feel effin' phenomenal.

I roll over to my right and don't feel a body next to me. Slightly concerned, but not alarmed, I keep reaching around. Nothing but air. Hmm?

I pry myself out of bed wondering where that tiger could be. Tough to get lost in a 1,000 square apartment. She's neither in the bathroom, nor the living room. I head to the kitchen. No one, but on the counter there's a cup of coffee and a note:

. . .

Christian,

So, you wanted to fuck me, huh? Now will you fight for me? Smile, it's a joke! You looked peaceful, so I didn't want to wake you. I had to run this morning. If you want to see me again, I'll be at the same place next Friday at 8pm. Come alone. Enjoy the cappuccino.
XO,
Liv

If I want to see her again? Is that even a real question? Of course I want to see her again. I'm kicking myself, though. How didn't I get her number? What the hell was I thinking? I didn't even give her my number. So dumb. What should I expect, though? I purposely didn't ask any questions. She looks like that, with the prowess of a wild cat in the bedroom. Plus, she's 41. Unless she's a murderer, there's no chance she's not with someone.

All the possibilities start to rise into consciousness. What if she is a spy? I am about to live like a real-life movie. What if she is married with kids? I am about to get shot by the husband. What if she is a lesbian? I am just some test rat or helping her live out some kind of fantasy. What if she's just single? Shit, would I actually date a 41-year-old? What would my Mother say? This is going to haunt me until next Friday. Best not to think about it. I don't even bother to call or text Jack. He'll just ask me a million questions, ones I'm not prepared to answer, and probably even try to convince me to keep it at one and done. Maybe that is the right call. Who knows? Time will tell, but there's zero chance I'm not going to see her again.

I try to spend Sundays with my parents, but I'm lucky if I get there twice a month. Sometimes my weekends get in the way, but it does help me silence the Sunday scaries and brace for Monday. Plus, Sundays are a big deal to my Mom, always have been, so I try to make it happen. My folks still live in the same house that I grew up in, a very small cape down in the Cove section of Stamford. It's only about ten minutes from my apartment.

My little brother Jacob lives out in California. He graduated from UC Berkeley and stayed out there. It's a different story every time you talk to him. Right now, he's working for some tech start-up in the valley. He's only 24. I don't worry about him, he's a bright kid, but naturally my parents do. I try to tell them an engineering degree from Berkeley is nothing to shake your tail at. He'll land on his feet one way or another. Hell, with any luck, maybe he'll become one of those tech millionaires.

Neither of my parents went to college. They're what you'd call risk averse. My Father, Douglas, is Scottish. Super frugal. He'll try to squeeze a dollar out of a rock. My Mother is Italian. Her name is Marie and she's exactly what every other Italian Mother named Marie is like: cooks a lot and Jacob and I can do no wrong in her eyes. Me, I'm American. I think identity by nationality is stupid. Who cares?

Actually, identity by anything other than me, Christian, the person people see in front of them, is pretty dumb. I actually hate my first name. Yes, I grew up Catholic. But I don't practice. It's like a dumb name for someone who isn't actually Christian. Whatever. Most people like it, that's a plus, I guess.

My Father worked in the construction union while my Mom stayed home to raise Jacob and me. I always joke with her that she needed something to do—that's why they had Jacob six years later. She is heartbroken that he's out in California, although she'd never admit it. My Father doesn't really give a shit. All that matters to him is that you have a job and you work hard every day.

I walk through their front door, it's about 2pm, and the screen slams shut behind me. I get a huge whiff of comfort coming from the kitchen. Spices and aromatic charm that would warm even the coldest heart. I look into the kitchen, and nobody is there. I yell out, "Mom! Dad! You home?"

"Christian, is that you?" Mom yells back. Her voice is coming from the small pantry off the kitchen. I can hear the TV playing in the background. That's the sound of Dad, in the living room toward the back of the house. Most of the time he's got the TV so loud you can hear it coming down the street.

"Yeah, Ma. It's me!"

She comes running out from the pantry with her cooking apron on. "So happy to see you, sweetie," she says. She opens up her arms, wraps them around me, and lays a big wet kiss on my cheek.

"Great to see you too, Ma," I say. "What's for dinner?"

She walks back to the kitchen to check on the stove. "Honey Dijon chicken. And I also made a roasted vegetable medley. Hm, some sweet potatoes. Oh, and some brown rice," she says with her back to me.

"No dessert?" I ask. She turns around with a strange look in her eye. As if I'm the crazy one.

"Of course. I made some chocolate chip cookies."

Dad's voice barks out from the back room, "Glad to see you made it, son."

I yell back, "Yup, just like every Sunday."

"Yeah, yeah. Every Sunday," he shouts. "Marie, does Christian make it every Sunday?"

Mom whispers to me, "Don't listen to him. I know

you're busy, dear." Then she yells to Dad, "Doug, dinner is almost ready, turn off the TV and come out here!"

"I'm coming, I'm coming."

I like to break my Father's balls and he's not shy to break mine right back. We've definitely had our bouts over the years. He can be a real pain in the ass at times. He's dead set in his ways, completely trapped in nostalgia, and has no patience for anything other than "the way it's always been done." I love my parents, but they're like medicine, good in the proper dose, too much may result in bodily harm.

At dinner, Dad is always to my right, sitting at the head of the table, and the kitchen behind him. Mom to his right, directly across from me, and the kitchen to her left. If Jacob were here, then he'd sit on my left. The table is big enough for two more, but we don't typically have any more guests. Maybe one day some grandkids. Mom is always quick to remind me of that. Right on cue, she asks, "So have you met anyone yet?"

I have no intentions of telling her about Liv, but since it is so fresh and illuminated in my mind, I think about it for a second or two. I know what Mom is really asking, "Are we closer to having any grandkids?" It's only natural for this to occur with aging parents. Think about it. For the longest time, I was the meaning in her life. Now that I'm self-sufficient, no longer in need of her, she is dying for something to do. She wants to relive mine and Jacob's childhood. Days at the ball field, arts and craft projects from school, and the holidays. She lacks meaning.

The whole kid thing always baffles me. People will literally force a relationship with someone they might not even be compatible with—just to have kids. That's the fascination we have with procreation. I couldn't even imagine having kids with someone I hate. Again, hang out with the after-4am crowd. It scares people straight. Just another lesson from the underworld. Actually, that's probably why there are so many screwed-up people in this world. They're a product, consummated by two people who just wanted kids, but didn't want to care for them. Oh, they got them alright. So did the world, now we have to deal with them.

I eat a bite of food and provide the standard answer, "Not yet, Mom. Chicken is delicious, though." Meanwhile, my Father sits there silently, pretending he's listening, but really he's just waiting to ask me the question he has in his mind.

"Why don't you have a girlfriend?" Mom asks. "Do you not want one?"

Here it is. That damn question again. Should I answer it honestly? The whole fuck-and-fight routine. The one I drew up in a weakened, dismantled, and shameful state and then doubled down on to melt Liv to the core? No way. I fire off another routine answer. "Because I haven't met anyone like you, Ma," I say. "That's why."

That gets Dad to break his silence with a laugh. "Be careful what you wish for," he says. "You might just get it."

Mom snaps her head to the left. "Oh, please," she says. "Like you're some saint."

Dad slams his fork down, takes a sip of water, and sighs. He looks at me and says, "This one, she can never take a joke."

"You know I'm sitting right here, Doug!?" Mom shouts.

"How can I possibly forget?"

Mom shakes her head and looks at me.

It's like: what the heck am I supposed to do? This is the effect of being married for 30 years or whatever. It's always something. If I have to listen to this all night, then I might as well just have the onus put back on me. I'd rather take the heat, so I stop eating for a minute. "Alright you two. Relax. You're both great. Can we just enjoy the dinner?"

We eat in silence for the next two minutes before Dad breaks it. "So Christian," he asks. "How's work going?"

This is the question he's been chomping at the bit to ask me. Always about work. Work. Work. Work. Before this, it was always baseball. Baseball. Baseball. Baseball. I wish I had our conversations on tape recorder. Even then, he would probably deny asking me about the same shit over and over. It's just Dad being Dad.

Honestly, baseball was pretty much my life growing up. I was kind of a natural athlete. I didn't need to work very hard to be good. I played Amateur Athletic Union as a kid and starting center fielder for all four years in high school. I was supposed to play at URI, but quit after my freshman year. There was a civil war in the Ballantine house when that happened. Dad hung his hat on the idea that his son was a good "ball player." I guess something to talk about with guys at the union.

I understand, for him, it was something to be proud about. The guy has been doing the same thing every day for the last 40 years, he keeps saying he's going to retire, but never does. I can't picture both of them home, doing nothing, all day long. God bless them both. Anyway, when you do the same thing every day, you learn to take pride in the smallest things. Otherwise, how do you wake up every day? So yes, me quitting baseball was an ordeal for him. Fast forward 12 years, now work is the big focus. The son with the high-paying sales job and taking the train into the city each day is the new baseball.

"Work is going really well. We have this awards event on Thursday," I say. "I'm up for the Rising Star Award. It's a big thing inside the company."

"Do you think you're going to win?" he asks. Then he

takes a bite of the chicken and, before I can respond, says, "I tell you what, this one knows how to cook though," as he points to Mom with a smirk on his face.

Mom just shakes her head and says, "Will you let Christian talk? You asked him a question."

I just sit there laughing to myself. "It's fine, Ma. Yes, I have a good shot," I say. "Pound for pound, I've got the best numbers in the office. Plus, I've slaved for this company for the last seven years and I think I deserve it. It would be great for my résumé."

"Well, you deserve it," Mom says. "You'll win. I'm sure of it." I wish I could carry her in my pocket all day.

I smile. "Thanks, Ma."

"All you can do is show up on time, work hard, and do your best. If you do that every day, then you've done your job. That's the way I see it," Dad says. "The rest is just smoke and mirrors. Either way, you've got a great job with great pay and great benefits and a roof over your head." It's such a Dad thing to say, but it's hard to argue with him.

We chat about the Yankees for a little while, break out the chocolate chip cookies, Mom clears the table, and Dad is snoring by 7pm. This is usually my out. I did my part, another Sunday in the books, and it's time to get out of here. Perfect timing, too. My muscles ache in all the wrong places, bones crack with every step, and emotions are running high. I'm susceptible to cry at a lonely kitten or snap at someone just for saying hello, never mind take any more of my folks. I'm dragging and I need some rest.

Monday morning is less than 12 hours away. The train, those costumes, and all the slugs at the office. It's time to face the slog.

FIVE

MONDAY WAS A BEAR, Tuesday was a drag, and Wednesday was a bitch. This week has been a long one, and it's only Thursday. Work felt like Woodstock in '69. I wasn't there, but I can imagine. Muddy dirty mess. All my coworkers were crying. Every client had an ass-ache, my boss's was the worst. He wanted everything done now. "Musta not have gotten laid this past weekend." Even the office admin looked like she hadn't been stuck right in a week. In fact, the only thing that got me through it was the thought of Liv.

All week my mouth was shut, but my mind was lucid. I could only dream. I couldn't wait for Friday, walking into the Fatty Duck, and seeing those blonde locks again. I'd find myself at my desk getting a chubby just thinking about it.

When you were a kid, they used to say, "Don't kiss and tell." Now I know why. All these rotten scoundrels start drooling over what's yours. They don't give a shit; they just want to daydream about her naked. The real ambitious ones will even make a move. Envy masks itself as fondness.

The jealous like to get close so it's easy to strike. Rip your heart to shreds and make your mind bleed. Me? I can handle it, but I wouldn't put Liv through that. She is someone who deserves some peace and quiet, but not in my mind. There, she is a seductress of the highest regard, ready to conquer the castle at any given moment.

But what am I thinking? I don't even know this woman. I know what she felt like and that was hard enough. People say warm apple pie—at least that's what I've heard. Liv felt more like pumpkin pie. A little more firm, a little less mushy. The only thing mushy, at times, was the way I saw her in my mind. And her preference in music left an aftertaste that's still lingering. It's keeping me sane this week, though. Thank God for daydreaming, otherwise I'd have to pay attention to Mark Undercuffler a little more often.

Undercuffler's the kiss-ass I gotta deal with on a regular basis. His lips are permanently attached to the cheeks of Mark Olson. They have some weird connection because they're both named Mark. Olson is our manager, he's got an important role, but he's just another layer in the shit sandwich that is corporate America. While managing the sales floor, he takes shit from upper management—VPs and the C-suite. He's caught between maniacs and greed heads. Powerless, except to the salespeople, so he'll exert that power every chance he gets.

Olson answers directly to the VP of Sales, Tim Alexander. He was brought in from an outside firm to help boost sales last year. When people get stepped over for an outsider, company employees frown on it, but Tim was supposedly some hotshot who helped grow a Fintech start-up from seed to going public.

I like outsiders, possibly another effect of hanging with the underworld; outsiders have moxie and fortitude.

Maybe that's why Tim and I have a good relationship. Well, as good as you can have with someone you don't see except for sales meetings, events, etc. His office is on the floor above mine with all the other VPs and C-suite executives. The higher up you get on the food chain, the more distant these people feel. They don't have a pulse on what's really going on. They rely on abstractions that echo out from the ground floor. By the time it gets to them, it's a watered-down vodka soda, the kind you get at the casino for free. I give Tim straight vodka when I see him. I think that's why he likes me.

Right on cue, I hear Undercuffler yell over from his desk, "Hey Christian. Did you get my email?"

In the time I've been with the company they've moved from cubicles to an open floor plan. It's supposed to promote community and collaboration or something. They're not fooling anyone, they did it to increase competition, everyone can hear everyone now. Supposed to make you sharper or something. If you ask me, it just promotes more chaos and stress. You already have a bunch of ego-driven, ex-athlete salespeople inside a building. We could barely focus before, even with the cubicles.

Companies play follow the leader, though. Oh, "they're'" doing it over there. Must be good for us. Let's just follow them off a cliff, too. Whatever makes you look good or "on it" is par for the course in corporate America. The cubicle decision falls in line perfectly.

Undercuffler has been after me the past two days because I took one of his "prospects," a potential piece of new business, out to lunch on Tuesday. The waters get murky with this stuff. We all have assigned geographical territories through management. The prospect has a shipping address here, a billing address there, and works in a completely different place. It's all bullshit. At the end of the day, the guy likes me, that's what should matter, that's why he wants to deal with me. But now I have to deal with the riot patrol.

"Yes, I got your email, Mark," I say. "What would you like to do? Sorry for any misunderstanding." The apology doesn't seem like it's going to be good enough.

"You know the rules, big guy," he yells across to me. I definitely have a stance for my position, so I got to play the game.

I hold ground and shout back, "No. I don't. Why don't you tell me, Mark?"

I put my head back into my computer for a moment, pretend like I'm typing, but I'm still listening. He stands up and yells, "Are you being a smart ass?"

I pick my head up slowly. "No, Mark. I just don't get what you're trying to do here. There's certainly some gray area in this situation." He's noticeably pissed, and all eyes are on us now. Everyone's distracted, two thumbs up for the open floor plan.

"Gray area? It seems pretty cut and dry to me," he yells. "Let's let Olson handle this!"

This isn't about to go my way and, worse, make me look like a conniving prick. So rather than battle it out in Olson's office, I pull an ace out of my sleeve and take the high road, sort of.

"Don't worry. I'll give the prospect to you," I yell over. "Check your email in 30. I'll make the email intro and BCC Olson so we're all on the same page."

I'm a man of my word. I do just that, but, like many things, the Devil is in the details. I email the prospect, tell him about the slight misunderstanding, and even talk up Undercuffler. I know the prospect will end up back on my desk.

Ultimately, it's the prospect's choice to work with

whoever they want. Sometimes they don't care about who they're dealing with; sometimes they do. Either way, it's their choice to work with you or your company. This could be due to a plethora of factors: the price is better, product is better, and on and on. But many times when you're trying to win competitive business—meaning: steal the business from your competitor—they're happy with their current situation. You are often the critical factor in winning that piece of business. The personal connection is everything. There are two things that matter more than anything in sales.

One is trust. Sure, companies work hard to build trust in the brand, brand loyalty, but in business-to-business selling, like my industry, financial data, you can throw brand loyalty out the window. Good data is good data. Cheap data is cheap data. So on and so forth. Personal connection —human connection—builds trust.

Two is likeability. In short: people work with people they like. If you're not likeable, you're not going to be very good at sales.

Undercuffler is great at what he does. We both came in during the same round of hires as associates seven years ago. Now we both put up some of the best numbers in the company. We've each made "Elite Club" for the last two years. It's a club you hit based on a certain benchmark of sales. It's the same benchmark for everyone. Every year, about 10% of the sales force gets Elite Club status. You get rewarded with a little bonus and trip on the company. Not too shabby. Anyway, Undercuffler is legit. He takes his job very seriously, which is why his lips are like suction cups. Politics is part of the game. That's his strategy. Here's mine.

Not even 15 minutes pass, and a one-line email comes back from the prospect, "No way. I'm out unless you're on the account, Christian." It would have been even better if the prospect replied all, but I can't have it all.

I forward that email to Mark squared. Immediately hear a grumbling, slam on the desk, Mount Undercuffler is about to erupt. "That's bullshit! This guy is stealing business," he shouts. "Ballantine, we're going to meet with Olson!"

Before I can even look up to say, "Fine," an email comes through from Olson, "Ballantine this is yours. You owe Undercuffler one."

The dynamics have changed. The prospect made his stance clear; he wants to work with me or all bets are off. There's no Director of Sales in the world who's going to side with Undercuffler in this situation. New business is new business. Olson is a puppet as much as he's our manager. He's got people to answer to and they demand a certain level of performance. Olson has to side with me. Plus, I look like the good guy because I did "try" to hand the prospect over. Risky move, but it worked—this time. Check mate, Undercuffler.

These are the political chess matches that get fought every day trying to climb the corporate ladder. Different scenarios, same characters. Whether I chose it consciously or unconsciously, it's the war I'm in, it's best to fight hard or you get trampled.

Next battle: tonight's award ceremony. If Undercuffler takes the crown, then I might end up calling Handley myself.

Thursday's workday comes to a close, the office starts to buzz about the awards dinner. It's an excuse for everyone to turn the water cooler talk into a poolside party. Time to rub shoulders with the higher-ups, everyone will be sure to have on their best costume.

SIX

THE AWARDS DINNER is always held during early March. Just enough time to not have already forgotten the previous year, but to also not disrupt the start of the new year. Smart move, I guess.

It's an ideal March evening. The stars are out, the moon is aglow, and there's a crisp breeze in the air. But rain or shine, warm or cold, the night won't be decided by the weather. I want to win that damn award.

The cocktail hour starts at 7pm. The dinner and awards start at 8pm. I'm going with the ol' fashionably late maneuver. Get in, get out. Win the award in between, shake a few hands, shine my pearly whites, and be back in Connecticut by 11pm. I can't let tonight get out of hand. Tomorrow is only one day away. I have been waiting all week to see Liv and I can't fuck that up. I strut through the door at 7.45pm, chest puffed out, wearing my superman costume.

This year's show is at The Bradbury in downtown Manhattan. Smallish venue with the feel of a men's club.

Low ceiling, brick walls, tufted leather couches, and subway tile floors. Modern art and metal figures hang from the walls. There's one quartz top bar in the back of the room serving top-shelf liquor while waiters walk the floor with hot and cold hors d'oeuvres. Everything from spiced meatballs to shrimp cocktail. It's the kind of room you want to smoke an Ashton and sip a single malt in. A perfect atmosphere to make you feel more important than you are. Well done, Perkins.

Everyone from the Manhattan office is at the event, including our CEO and Founder Ellison Perkins. People close to him call him EP. He's an old-school guy. Sinatra, card games, and dark liquor. He started the company in 1974 and, 36 years later, he's a billionaire. There's a bit of an aura that follows him around. I mean, it's his company, the legend of EP is stamped all over the place. His quotes are on the walls in the office, origin story is in every company pamphlet, and war stories that sound more like tall tales are passed along by employees. The billionaire founder who started with nothing.

Anyway, tonight smart employees are on their best behavior, but the associates stumble around all night taking advantage of the free booze. This is just another corporate booby trap if you ask me. These events are just as much a gauntlet as they are a party. You never know who you'll be stuck in a conversation with or what mask you're going to have to wear.

I don't even get my first drink before I hear, "Oh, Ballantine. Good to see you." It's Tim Alexander. He seems to already have a few in him.

"Ah, Tim. Likewise. How's everything up on the 44th floor?" He gives me a half-smile.

"Good. I'm settling in nicely. We had a good year," he

says, then puts his hand on my shoulder. "Big part of that was you. Don't think that's gone unnoticed."

"Oh yeah? How well-noticed? Rising Star Award noticed?"

His smile turns into a laugh. "Honestly, I'm announcing the award and I don't even know the winner," he says. He's only one vote of six that determine the award, so I know he's not lying. With his hand still on my shoulder, he leans over to my left ear. "I didn't tell you this but . . . " he pauses "You got my vote."

I stand there stone cold, hiding my excitement, and take a sip of my Tom Collins. "Thanks, Tim. That means a lot to me," I say.

Tim pulls his hand off my shoulder and fixes his eyes on me. "Listen, you deserve it."

I slam down the rest of my drink. Is tonight my night? Sure feels like it.

Before I can soak in that good vibe, I feel someone sneak up behind me and whisper, "You might have got me today, but I'm going to get you tonight." I instantly know who it is. I can tell from the sound of his voice. It's just the kind of bullshit you'd expect from Undercuffler. Before I can respond, he steps around and faces me. "What's going on Ballantine?" he says. "Dateless as usual?"

Always with the lame-ass jokes. Like a fuckin' date matters to me. Another favorite joke of his is when a client or prospect asks if I have kids. "Well, not that he knows about," he likes to say.

Undercuffler's wife is standing next to him, Molly. I've I met her a few times over the years. I take the opportunity to razz him back. "I'm happy to see you found at least one woman who can deal with you," I say. "Pleasure to see you, Molly. How's everything?"

Molly seems too sweet for Undercuffler, but what do I know? She could be a raging maniac behind closed doors. On second thought, she's just the type of girl who ends up with an Undercuffler, a dreams-of-1950-America type. White picket fence, stay-at-home Mom, three kids, and hot dinner served at 6pm on the dot every night. Honey, I'm home.

Undercuffler butts in, "We just had our first baby!"

"Right, right," I say. "All is well?"

Molly shakes my hand.

"Thank you," she says. "It's been great, a lot to handle, but great."

"I can only imagine," I say. "Well, congrats and good health."

Of course, Olson isn't too far behind Undercuffler. Another member of the married and miserable club. He's looking jolly tonight, though. He shouts, "Ballantine! It's good to see you. Are you ready for a fun night?"

I just nod my head. "Oh yeah, Olson. Ready for some fun." Then I grab a glass of Champagne from the waiter's tray as he walks by.

"You remember my wife Claire, right?" he asks.

I've literally met her at every work event the last seven years. "Yes, I remember. Pleasure to see you, Claire. You look great tonight."

"Thank you, Christian," she says. "Always a pleasure to see you too."

Olson points over to the dinner area. "Looks like everyone is heading in," he says. "We should make our way over."

"Just need to use the head. Be over in five," I tell him.

I need to regroup for a minute. Plus, I actually have to drain the lizard, re-tuck my shirt, and hike up my slacks.

No bathroom visit is complete without splashing some water on the face. I notice this place has my favorite cologne. Too many good signs, it's starting to make me nervous, well, at least I'll smell good. I take a few spritzes and pop a mint in my mouth. Let's do this. I pull the bathroom door open with force, spin around the corner, and head to the dining room with a bold strut.

The room that was filled with people for cocktail hour is now empty aside from one female standing there with long blonde hair. She appears to either be lost or looking for someone. It's on step number three that I get hit with a mallet that knocks me back to last week. My knees quiver, heart trembles, and I can't see straight. I recognize that silhouette. "Liv, is that you?"

She turns her head around. "Christian!?"

Liv is dressed for the occasion, looking stunning, and standing alone in the middle of the room. Her look goes from spirited to stern in the blink of an eye. Her elation turns to nervousness. I can't even get a word out.

Tim comes jogging out from the dining room. "Honey, I'm so happy you made it on time," he says. "Dinner is just about to start. C'mon let's go."

As Tim leans in to hug Liv my heart goes from a tremble to a dead stop. When he pulls back to give her a peck on the lips, I can't believe it. Am I dreaming right now?

Not even a second later, Tim spots me. "Christian? C'mon, they're about to start," he says with a raised voice. "Oh, and this my wife, Olivia. Christian is one of the most talented salespeople in the company."

I can barely speak, so I clear my throat. "Pleasure to meet you Li . . . " I clear my throat again. "Sorry, I had a mint stuck in my throat!" It was the best I could come up with. "Pleasure to meet you, O-livia." I can't believe it.

Tim laughs.

"Likewise," Liv says. "You look dashing tonight, Christian."

It's a sultry, tempting, and seductive thing to say. She seems like she knows what she's doing. I get the sense that she might even like the danger. Personally, I'm scared shitless.

Tim chimes in, "Let's get in there!"

The awards ceremony begins over dinner. Undercuffler and I are at the same table. Tim and Liv are sitting diagonally from me at a separate table. They're with Olson, Claire, and some others from upper management. I can see Tim's arm around Liv and each time she turns to look at him, I get flashbacks. I see Liv's hair draped over one eye, looking back at me, and willingly taking me thrust after thrust. The vision gets cut short by Tim's voice in my head, "You got my vote." I try to continue, but that voice keeps speaking. "Christian is one of the most talented salespeople in the company."

What have I done? I can barely swallow the prime rib, but the gin is going down easier and easier. The combination of Liv and alcohol makes me a mute. I can't even make table conversation. I am a silent salesman, antisocial, and perspiring in the heat of the moment. The mental chatter is too distracting. All I can hear, over and over again, is: holy shit, holy shit, holy shit.

The awards start, but things appear to be moving in slow motion. I'm clapping and smiling. The room is noiseless, faces are laughing, and my fork is going in and out of my mouth. It's like a scene from a silent movie. Is this what shock is like? I look at Undercuffler and he has horns growing out of his head. Is he the Devil? Is this hell?

The spell is broken by an "Ahem!" that comes over the loudspeaker. I look up and Tim is at the podium at the front of the room. "Ahem," he clears his throat again. "Sorry about that. So, I've had the pleasure of being here for just over a year." His voice snaps me back to reality. "We've had a tremendous year and I want to thank all of the hardworking salespeople who made this happen. We couldn't do this without each and every one of you. As you know, probably better than I, the Rising Star Award is given to one salesperson in the company who not only performs at the highest level, but we feel has an extremely bright future at Perkins."

While Tim talks, I find myself stealing glances at Liv's perfectly shaped shoulders. It's easy to do, as her eyes are fixed on the podium. Tim magnifies his voice and it grabs my attention.

"Now I want to start a new tradition moving forward," he says. "Many of you probably don't know this, but I have a vacation home down in Florida."

EP yells out, "Wow—I didn't know we were paying you that much." It gets a rise out of everyone in the audience. Tim laughs along.

"Maybe that came out a little wrong," he says. "If you let me finish, what I was trying to say was: as a show of appreciation for the winner of the Rising Star Award, I will be hosting you for a weekend of relaxation, right outside of Miami, in the little town of Golden Beach." There are lots of "Oooos" from the crowd. It's an even blend of sarcasm and appreciation.

One guy yells out, "Do you have to come?"

Tim chuckles, then says, "Good one."

I snag another quick look at Liv, and she appears to be relishing the razzing of Tim. I can't turn my head back toward the podium fast enough. Liv looks back, our eyes cross, but she keeps hers moving. Shit, I'm caught staring. She flips her hair, turns her head, and places her attention back on Tim. What does she expect? Why look if you didn't want to see me, Liv?

"Pipe down, pipe down," Tim says over the microphone. He picks up an envelope from the podium and tears it open. "Now . . . this year's winner of the Rising Star Award is. . . " He pauses and takes a breath. " . . . actually, it looks like we're going to have a full house this year! We've got co-winners!" Tim looks up toward the crowd, "Mark Undercuffler and Christian Ballantine—congratulations, you're both Rising Stars this year!"

I can't tell if I don't want to get up or I can't. The floor turns to quicksand, some stupid rock song starts playing, and everyone is clapping. I should be ecstatic right now, but everything else has spoiled the moment. I'm stuck on Liv being Tim's wife and now I've got to share the award with Undercuffler and go on a trip with him and Tim? What the hell is happening? Molly reaches over and taps me on the shoulder. "Go up," she mouths, and I nod. Undercuffler is already striding in front of me like a thoroughbred about to take the triple crown. I get up and begin my slow walk to the podium.

Christian Ballantine, the man of many thoughts, is finally thoughtless. Drawing a dead blank, I see a hand reach out, so I shake it. I hear a man say, "Congratulations, son. Good work. Your future is bright here." My God, it's EP.

I nod and smile. "Thank you, Sir."

I get up front and shake Tim's hand, and his grip is firm. He yells, "Nice work!" and gives me a gold plaque to commemorate the award. Undercuffler is standing next to Tim already with his plaque in hand. All three of us turn toward the crowd. Tim is standing between us with his arms draping around our shoulders. The cameraman pops off a few shots. Flash, flash, flash.

As the light from the camera starts to vanish, I see two sparkling green lights coming from the center of the room. I squint and look closer. They're Liv's eyes smiling at me. The mantra starts up again in my head: holy shit, holy shit, holy shit.

SEVEN

THE NEXT MORNING, I arrive at the Perkins building on Park Ave, nod at the doorman, and shine him a cheesy smile.

"Good morning, Sir," he says.

As I step through the revolving door, I wonder if "Sir" is too polite a greeting for me this morning, but herein lies the power of a smile. Fake or not. People hide behind smiles every day.

The elevator can't come fast enough. I press the up button at least three times, as if that will make it come quicker. It doesn't and I'm still rubbing my eyes. Overall, I slept maybe two hours. I kept thinking about all the dynamics that make this situation a nightmare. Most obviously, I slept with the boss's wife. Worse, I'm supposed to see her tonight. Even worse, he likes me, I kind of like him, and even worse than that—I'm about to spend the weekend with him at his beach house. Should I even go to see Liv tonight?

Ding. The elevator door opens, and I step inside.

The muzak reminds me of the car ride home last

night. Who picks elevator muzak, anyway? I took off shortly after I won the award. It was the loneliest car ride I can remember. Tom Waits was the perfect music for the quiet and somber drive. I must have listened to the song 'I Hope I Don't Fall in Love with You' a dozen times. I got stuck in traffic on I95 which made the ride even longer. Construction, like always. Good thing, though, the blinking lights were a reminder that I was still conscious. I thought about everything from calling Handley, to texting Jack to meet for a drink, to stopping at some random strip club. I needed some stimulation to kill the pain. A cooler head prevailed, though. I got lost in thought for two hours, and made it home in one piece.

Ding. The elevator door opens, and I step onto the office floor.

I walk out, take a left, and greet the office admin, Nicole. She looks like she might have had one too many at the event. "Good to see you this morning," I say. "Did you have a nice time last night?"

"A little tired this morning—ha," she says. "I guess that means I did. Congratulations on that award."

I tap the counter in front of her. "Thanks, Nicole. Thanks."

There are not many people in the office this morning. Neither Undercuffler nor Olson are in yet. Did I miss a memo or something? I look at my watch, *What the . . . ?* It's only 8am. I hope I'm not losing my mind. While in motion to put my briefcase on my desk, I see a sticky note that reads:

Come see me first thing this AM. I'm in early. - Tim

. . .

I never get summoned to the 44th floor. Fuck, I knew I'd be walking on pins and needles, but as soon as I come through the door? C'mon! Tim usually comes down to see me or us on our floor, the 43rd. Did Liv tell him about us? Shit, if she did, what do I say? I feel a slight perspiration above my lip. I head to the water cooler, down two cups, loosen my tie, and take a deep breath, resting my arm on the jug. I'd rather be waterboarded than deal with this conversation right now.

In my mind, I start rehearsing what I'll say, "Seriously, I didn't even know Liv was your wife. I was drunk. It was a one-time thing. It'll never happen again." Sounds believable? Shit, I want to see her again. Do the right thing, Christian. Do the right thing. Maybe I'll just say, "I'm so sorry. I had no idea that Olivia was your wife." Perfect. Leave it vague and totally honest. How could he get mad at that? Well, I did screw his wife. But definitely say Olivia, no nicknames.

I look at my watch and it reads 8.15am. God forbid this gets ugly. I should probably get up there before everyone gets in. I walk into the elevator, press 44, put my head down and, before I can pick my head up, the door slides open. Did it even close? I peek out: shit, it's definitely the 44th floor.

This space is a little different from the sales floor. It's all individual offices around the outside with a conference room in the middle. All glass, too. Everyone can see everyone. Each office has their own secretary, and they're all here this morning getting things organized before their bosses come in.

Tim's secretary is named Lorelei. She's an attractive woman in her 30s, brown hair, big bust, small waist, and wearing flats. The brief distraction is nice, but in my peripheral I see Tim typing away at his computer. He looks up, sees me, and raises his arm to signal me over. Act cool, Christian. Cool and confident. Don't forget to thank him again. I grin and lift my hand to signal I see him.

"Good morning, Tim," I say once I get to his door.

He finishes typing something. "You're here early," he says. "Have a seat." I slide into one of the leather chairs in front of his desk.

"Yeah. I just wanted to get going early today."

Still typing, he says, "You had fun last night?"

"It was a good time," I reply. He seems to be paying more attention to the screen than he is to me.

"We all got a little tipsy," he says. "So we told everyone to come in a little later today."

I put two and two together. "Ah, I was wondering why the office was a bit empty. I took off pretty early last night."

Tim smirks and says, "I noticed that. No biggie." He continues to type away and squint into the screen. "Why'd you duck out so early?"

My brain starts to rip through reasons. I settle on, "Um. Ya know, I was just tired. I live in Stamford." That comment makes his ears perk up, he stops typing, and fixes his eyes on me. "CT, huh? Same here! I live in Greenwich."

I can feel beads of sweat starting to seep through under my arms.

"You didn't miss much," he continues. "So, you probably want to know why I wanted to see you first thing . . . "

I jump the gun a bit and blurt out, "I just want to tell you . . . " at the same moment he continues, " . . . Well, I just want to give you some details . . . " We both stop in our tracks.

Tim speaks first, "What were you going to say?"

I gulp, then say, "Sorry, didn't mean to cut you off."

"No, go ahead," he says.

"I just want to tell you . . . how thankful I am for the award last night. It means a lot to me."

"Christian, it was my honor. You deserve it. That's exactly why I called you up," he says. "I wanted to give you some details on the trip to Golden Beach." I feel the weight of a sumo wrestler come off my shoulders.

"Yes, of course," I say. "I love South Florida. I've had some *good* nights in Miami."

Tim laughs. "I'm sure. It's a fast town. My wife and I love it down there. That's why I bought the place two years back."

"Oh really? It's pretty new for you then."

"Yeah it is . . . "

I get fixated on a photo that I spot directly over his right shoulder and zone out for a minute or two. It's a photo of Liv and a young girl. Who is that? Does she have a daughter? Am I a homewrecker? This would make the situation even more fucked up. I want to ask him about the photo, but I don't want her name to come up. Avoiding her name at all costs is the objective.

I start to hear Tim's voice again, " . . . thoughts?"

Shit, I missed everything he just said. I sit there for a moment.

Tim chimes back in, "Did you hear me?"

I wipe my eyes. "Ah sorry. Haven't had my coffee yet." Tim laughs again.

"What I said was the place is decent size. Plenty of bedrooms. Four, actually. I spoke with Undercuffler after you cut out last night and he'll be bringing Molly. Olivia and I make four. You got anyone you want to bring? Thoughts?"

Liv is coming to Golden Beach!? This is bad. Real bad. Much worse than I thought.

"When are we leaving?" I ask.

"Yeah. A date would be good," he says, then looks at the calendar. "We're leaving in a couple weeks. Dates are March 20 to 23. Friday to Monday. Don't worry about vacation days for any of those dates. This one is on the company. We're going to celebrate."

Who the heck drops a trip on someone only a couple weeks away? Is he making this hard on purpose? Does he know about Liv? Fuck. Stop being crazy. He doesn't know. He would say something. Two weeks is plenty of notice.

Clearly, I have no one to bring, but I can't not go. That's like a slap in the face. Plus, I can't let Undercuffler have one-on-one time with Tim. Not for four days, no fucking way. His nose will be so far up Tim's ass he'll be able to smell his breath.

Tim saves me. "Look, I know you're not exactly tied down," he says. "I was your age once and, believe it or not, I see a lot of you in me. I didn't get married until I was 39. I know you're just having fun right now."

I can't decide if I want him to continue or stop. Me, like him? It's flattering and jarring at the same time. Is that why Liv slept with me? Does she see Tim in me too?

Tim continues, "Anyway, I have an extra bedroom. So, feel free to bring a buddy or something. Just no whores. Olivia will be on my ass."

When you're in sales you learn to laugh even when shit isn't funny. This was one of those moments. "No whores? That would be fun." He laughs too.

"No whores," he repeats.

There's only one buddy I can bring—Jack. But do I really want him there? He knows about Liv and doesn't know about this situation—yet. Hmm, any others?

Ava? Nope, whore. Sofia? Not a whore, but haven't talked to her in months. She'll get the wrong idea.

Margaret? Who the hell is named Margaret? Terrible name, no way. Angelica? Nope, def whore. Screw this, I can trust Jack.

"I might bring my buddy Jack," I say. "If you don't mind, I know it's not a date, exactly."

Tim starts to laugh, then stops. "All good," he says.

"I just have to ask him later this morning."

Tim raises his finger. "Oh, and use your corporate AMEX for flights, parking, and taxis. This is on us," he says.

"What about Jack? I mean, should I use the card for him, too, if he comes?"

He grins. "Who approves your expense report?"

"Olson."

"And who approves Olson's?" Tim says.

"You?"

"Exactly. Don't worry about it. Yes, expense him if he comes with you. Undercuffler is doing the same thing for Molly, anyway."

There's no way Jack won't come, this deal is too sweet for him, paid trip to Miami. Well, 20 minutes out on the A1A, but same shit.

Tim looks at his watch, then back toward me. "One last thing. Arrive any time after 2pm on the 20th. That's when I'll be there. The address is 369 Centre Island, Golden Beach. Don't worry about confirming Jack. He comes or not, doesn't matter to me."

"Thanks, Tim. Really nice of you."

"My pleasure," he says, pointing over to the door. "Okay. Now go sell something. Let's get some work done."

I get back to my desk and I realize it's still only 8.40am. Too early to text Jack, but early enough to ease into the day before the circus freaks arrive. I grab a coffee from the instant coffee maker in the hall, power on my computer, sit back in my chair, flip through my planner, and check what I have on the calendar.

Shit, today is Friday. The day I've been waiting for all week, now marred by an evolving situation, what a disaster. Should I even go to the Fatty Duck tonight? Will Liv even show up?

EIGHT

I was hoping today would go by slow. Nope. It took off like a rocket and never let up. Once I got fixated on tonight's dilemma, I just couldn't shake it. It was like listening to one of those radio pop jams, manufactured to play in your mind on repeat, the one you find yourself singing tomorrow morning in the shower. Actually, the dilemma is more like wet cement. You can get rid of wet cement before it dries, but, once it hardens, you're fucked. The dilemma dried and hardened. I've been fucked all day.

Plus, I've been dancing somewhere between gratitude and envy with my coworkers. That's the funny thing about winning an award or getting some recognition. They build you up to tear you down. Nobody cares as much as I do, and, apparently, I don't even care as much as I thought I did. I'm walking around with a target on my back, but for what? Career progression? I slept with the boss's wife. How the hell am I doing?

Coworkers will tell you they're proud of you. Only naive children could believe that rubbish. They'll say congratulations and give you a pat on the ass, but behind that plastic smile is dragon breath ready to burn your life to the ground at any moment.

Never mind Undercuffler, a real-life Roger Klotz plotting his next move with every step I take. Who, by the way, will be in Florida with me, Tim, and Liv. This situation is more dangerous than dynamite. I could leave missing a limb, or worse, with no job. Jobless people don't get laid, do they? Only with other jobless people, I'm guessing.

At least Jack texted me that he's coming. Thank God. I need some citrus to cut the heat. He doesn't know about the entire situation yet, but he'll find out soon enough. I cut out of work early to grab coffee with Jack. I have to rip my costume off and let Christian breathe. So, I leave a note for Olson:

Client meeting. See you Monday. - CB

Olson never breaks my balls for leaving the office early, so shorter the note the better. It comes with the territory of being a top performer; he lets me be. And, what am I going to say? "Hey, I had to bounce because I can't stop thinking about Tim's wife. Oh, and by the way I banged her, and now I need to go and deliberate with my good friend Jack on whether I should go see her again tonight." No, that's too much, too Christian, work needs less Christian, more costume.

I pull into the coffee shop and see Jack is waiting for me inside with a cup already in front of him. Finally, a pleasant surprise. This never happens. I can see him playing around on his phone through the window. I hop out of the car, he sees me and sneers, I sneer back. We both know something is up, or maybe he's just in a good mood. I hope the latter, because I need some advice from the last person who's qualified to give it.

I swing the door open and shout, "Hey, citrus!" He looks up startled and confused, but grinning.

"Citrus, what?"

I start laughing. "Don't worry. I hope that coffee is strong."

"Oh Christ," he says. "What now?"

So, I tell him the entire story from start to finish. All the dynamics of the trip. Liv's real name is Olivia. She's Tim's wife. Tim likes me. I had sex with Liv. I didn't know, but now I do. The awards dinner. The win. The trip with both of them. Oh, and the Undercuffler effect. All that good stuff.

Jack takes a sip of coffee and asks, "Why didn't you tell me about Liv earlier?"

What a selfish prick. People always make stuff about them. "The week got busy, then I had the award ceremony last night," I reply. "Forget that. I just need some damn guidance here!"

The real reason is: I thought I liked Liv. Correction. I do like her. I didn't want Jack to spoil it with his heartless poison telling me she's old and not my type. You know, all that bullshit that comes along when you say, "I think I really like her, dude." Even if Jack's divorce left him jaded, he's still a human parasail that glides through life. The blowing wind only makes him go faster.

"I'll tell you what to do," he says. He's got my full attention. He takes a sip of coffee. "Don't bang her again." Shit, I was afraid he was going to say that.

Jack continues, "Dude. I've been Liv before. You know, the cheater. Well, I didn't stop and not because I hated my wife or because I didn't want to. It just felt too good. I wanted that lust every day. I'd wake up to normalcy, my wife, the house, our life and then there was that other life. It was new, dangerous, and thrilling. I couldn't help myself. So, why am I telling you this? Because Liv *ain't* going to stop, she's going to tell you she wants to, but she won't. Why? Because she'll never be able to shake the thrill." He takes another sip of his coffee and looks out the window nearby. "She ain't going to stop until her whole world crashes and burns. Just like me. Except you're going to be left in that rubble. Dust all over your face, looking around hoping you still got a job."

I look up at the ceiling, and Jack laughs.

I look back down and sigh. "You're probably right. Here's the real conundrum. After our night together, she took off before I got up and left a note on my kitchen table. She said if I wanted to see her again, I had to meet her tonight at the Fatty Duck at 8pm. So, should I go or not even bother?"

He almost spits out his coffee. "Is that a serious question? You have to go. You can't let the next time you see her be in Florida. You got to clear the air. You got to end it and make sure she's on the same page as you. Otherwise all bets are off."

I drag my fingertips from my forehead to chin leaving red streaks, and sit there silent. I know he's right. "You alright, dude?" Jack asks. I nod.

"I'll tell you what, though," he says. "She is hot and made her friend Emma look like Swiss cheese. That's why I had to get out of there."

Emma was actually good looking, but he's right, it's all relative. Emma might have been pretty, but that night she was just the woman next to Liv. That's the problem with our brains.

I look out the window and look back at Jack. I know

what I have to do. Jack stares back at me with a shit-eating grin and shrugs. I nod to let him know we're on the same page.

"So, how's the house?" he asks. "Is it sick?"

I can only grin back. "Yeah, Jack. It's sick."

NINE

A SENSE OF CALM comes over me as I get ready. The conversation with Jack really helped to relax my nerves. It's amazing how talking to someone can do that for you. I feel like a trained prize fighter heading into a boxing match. My only unease comes at the thought of the other fighter. Will Liv even show up? If she does, what is her game plan? How's she been training?

I spend more time than usual to ensure everything is just right with my appearance. Probably a stupid idea, but an honest one. My vanity is shining through in full force. I mean, I can't go down looking like a mess. I want to stain her mind. Last time I saw her, she said I looked dashing. Tonight, I am shooting for sizzling.

As I comb my hair, lotion my body, and brush my teeth, I focus on what I have to do. It's the only viable choice—end it.

I pull up to the Fatty Duck at 7.45pm and walk inside. I'm 15 minutes early. It's another cool March evening. The place is buzzing with a dinner crowd. Typical for a Friday. The only TV that hangs in the bar is playing a hockey game. A late season match-up between New York Rangers vs New Jersey Devils. No volume. DJ isn't here yet. All you can hear is the banter of patrons. A few cheering the hometown Rangers, others ordering drinks and making small talk.

I begin to look around for Liv, even though I don't expect her to be here early. Not surprised, I don't see her. Luckily, I find an open seat at the bar on the far side. I walk through the dining area rather than around the U to get the open stool, just to make sure Liv isn't already sitting down somewhere. The fire in the fireplace gives the place a cozy feel. It's smoky, woody, and comforting. Perfect for a chilly evening. It's much quieter on this side of the place. You can hear the sound of the kitchen door opening and closing. The only real noise spills over from the bar area.

I get to the barstool and quickly realize how perfect it is. I'm directly facing the entrance.

The same bartender from the week before is working. She recognizes my face. "Hey you, here alone tonight?"

I play it cool. "I'm that obvious, huh?"

She smiles.

"Right now. But maybe meet up with someone in a short while. Figured I'd catch some of the game," I say.

"Rangers look good. 2-0 in the middle of the second," she says. "What are you having?"

I don't want to drink before I see Liv. Alcohol does a number on your emotions, but I can't just sit here. Plus, that doesn't align so well with the ever-so-slight lie I just told. Fuck it.

"Tom Collins," I say.

She points at me. "Right! Tom Collins."

"Yes. You remember!"

"A good bartender never forgets," she says. She starts to

mix my drink and I notice she uses a sugar cube rather than simple syrup.

"Is that the trick?" I ask.

"What?" she replies.

"Sugar cube rather than simple syrup."

"Simple syrup is typically less sweet, but it's also a compound, a mixture of water and sugar. If I can use each ingredient individually, I do. It helps me control the consistency," she says.

"Touché. I'll buy that."

It's 8pm on the nose. Liv should be here any minute. I'm pretending to watch the game, but I'm on a bed of nails waiting for her to walk through the door. I feel like Tony Soprano watching the diner entrance in the series finale. Am I about to get whacked? Each time the door opens, a cool draft blows across the room, my heart skips a bit thinking it might be her, and I can hear Jack say, "Don't bang her again."

It's ten past eight and my drink is already getting low. Do I order another? No way. I'll never stand up to the fire. I'll melt like ice cream in the summer. The bartender looks at me. "Another?"

"Sure. Why not?" I say, astonished at my weakness. I see the front door open again, and finally; there she is. She came. Standing there, looking around. Should I make her sweat it out? Nah. I raise my hand, she sees me, smiles, and begins to walk over.

"So, you decided to show up?" she says, beating me to the punch.

"Funny. I was about to say the same thing to you."

It doesn't take her long to start flirting. "You look great, as always."

"And, by 'always,' you mean the two times you've seen me? Unless, of course, you're stalking me."

She hits my shoulder. "Right!"

I've seen her three different ways before tonight: casual with her hair pulled back, stunning in formal wear, and, well, naked. I'd gladly take her in all three. Tonight, though, she has an edgy look to her. At first I can't tell, but when I offer her my seat at the bar, she takes her overcoat off, and lays it on the back of the chair. It reveals a couple rips in the knees of her jeans, black leather bomber, and heeled boots. All complementing her darker make-up and messy blonde hair.

Liv orders a martini, and I stand there nursing my second cocktail while hovering at her right side. The real conversation hangs over our heads like a dark cloud. I look to savor the last moments of sunlight, but I can't resist the sound of thunder in my mind.

"So . . . I have to ask you. Did you know? Did you know I work for your husband?"

She looks back in awe. "Wow," she says. "Absolutely not."

I didn't mean to offend her, but I do want to know. "I'm sorry. I didn't mean it like that. You just have to admit it's the *craziest* coincidence ever," I say.

She looks down at her drink, then at me. "Yes, it is." She takes a sip and continues, "Did *you* know I was married to Tim?"

Her cleverness strikes me, I clam up for a second, and sputter. "Funny, Liv. No, I didn't even know you were married. Let alone to my freaking boss!"

"Oh, please," she snaps back. "We both know you didn't want to know any details about me. If you did, would it have even mattered?" I sit there in silence for ten seconds which feels more like ten minutes.

She nudges me. "Huh, would it?"

I have no choice but to answer honestly and shamefully. "No, probably not."

Except when I say it, I'm not feeling very shameful, but I am being honest. I want her to know that those thin, well-manicured fingers have a grip on my pulsing, mushy heart. It was that damn grip that left indents all week long. I was alone, but she was with me everywhere I went. Now, face to face, I have plenty of questions to ask her.

"I don't know how to say this without you getting mad," I say. "Will you promise me you won't get mad?"

Liv sighs. "Yes, I promise."

I stir my drink three or four times. "I probably shouldn't ask you this, but Tim said something to me that I just can't shake. It's driving me nuts, actually." I pause for a half-second. "He said I reminded him of him. Is that why you were attracted to me?"

Her face turns red, maybe upset, but visibly possessing the look of a whimper. "Christian. Do you mind if we get out of here?"

"Out of here? We just got here."

"I just don't want to have this conversation in a crowded bar."

I do understand, but she did just avoid answering the question. I don't even know why I care so much about it. I guess I just want to know. It would make sense if she thought I was a younger version of him.

"Where do you want to go?" I ask.

She downs the martini in one clean swoosh, places the empty glass on the table, tightens her lips, and furrows her brow. "How about the ice cream shop down the street?"

"Ice cream? It's so cold."

"If you're not the type of person who can eat ice cream all year round, then you've got bigger problems."

I can't help but laugh.

"Ice cream or not?" she asks.

"Okay, okay," I say. "Ice cream it is."

Walking to the ice cream shop, I don't know what to expect. March is a mysterious month; you never know what the weather will bring. Tonight, the moon is full and bright enough to light up the chalk-colored clouds. I don't ask any questions during the walk. I watch our breath leave a trail in the night sky. It's a stolen moment of happiness in a precarious situation. A reminder that we're only human.

I open the ice cream shop door for Liv and a little bell jingles. There is no one in here except two young girls working behind the counter. Perhaps the hidden benefit of going to get ice cream in the winter, a secret reserved for just Liv and me.

"You see, I closed the whole place just for us," I say. She can't hide the smile, although she visibly tries.

"So, what will you have?" I ask her. She takes a minute and looks at the chalkboard hanging behind the counter. You can barely make out the handwritten flavors in a variety of pastels.

Just like a kid at the schoolyard, she looks at me with a girlish smile, and says, "Vanilla ice cream, hot fudge, dollop of whipped cream, and a cherry on top."

"So an ice cream sundae?"

"Yeah."

We both smirk. It's the most classic ice cream order. Even the cherry, I mean, I hear people say that dumb cliché—cherry on top—all the time, but I can't remember the last time I actually saw someone get the cherry on top.

"Do I have to say the word dollop?" I ask her.

"Yes, of course, anymore would be too much and any less would be not enough."

I can tell she's playing with me, but I like it. There are Styrofoam cups on the counter, they remind me of a milk-shake, so I get a coffee one. Styrofoam is perfect to shield your hands from the cold, especially on an already chilly evening.

There are only a few tables in the narrow shop, all tucked along the wall, we choose the last one in the row. Liv sits with her back to the door, while I look directly at it. The big windows in front show me the moonlit sky, a perfect backdrop to look at Liv. It's the ideal contrast for her natural radiance.

I don't feel Liv is avoiding moving forward in our discussion as much as I feel she is relishing the moment. But my anxiety is beginning to creep up again. After all, it is me who is in the worse predicament. I want to continue the real conversation, but I don't have to say anything. I think Liv senses what I am thinking.

"This is why I was attracted to you," she says.

"What?"

"You came to the ice cream shop," she says. "Sure, you gave me a little pushback, *but* we came. You even made a joke when we walked in."

"So that's why you were attracted to me?"

"You are handsome, okay, you are sexy, so I am physi-cally attracted to you. But you're also playful," she says. "Soo, when you asked me if you were like Tim it reminded me that Tim isn't playful. That made me sad."

I don't really know what to say next, so I just say the first thing that comes to mind. "So, I'm not like Tim?"

She looks dead at me. "Don't be silly."

I'm still confused. Does she think I'm joking with her? But I just roll with the moment. I take a slurp of my milkshake then smile at her with coffee ice cream all over my teeth.

She blurts, "You see, that's what I mean! Tim would never do that."

I find myself in a weird spot, defending Tim. "Right, but Tim is also 49 and I'm 30."

She takes a bite of her sundae, licks the back of the spoon, and pauses for a moment. Just enough time for me to pretend like that spoon is . . . She cuts back in before I can finish the thought.

"When I met Tim, I was about your age and we got married two years later. He was charming, good looking, and wore a Patek Philippe." She laughs to herself, then continues, "Tim was many things, but never playful. And people don't change, Christian. They just learn to adapt, to survive. I was hypnotized by the thought of finally settling down and having a real future with someone who had a foundation. Someone I could start a family with. I lived a very playful life before I met Tim. I went to concerts, traveled, and, well, experienced many things. I've had a lot of experiences."

She laughs again. Liv is a minx. I've seen it in her eyes and, heck, I've been to bed with her. I'd done the same thing for the last ten years. Who am I to judge?

"So, when I met you, Christian," she says. "It took me back to those years prior to Tim. I felt something I hadn't in a long time. I felt alive."

At that moment, Jack flashes into mind. It's kind of like what he was trying to suggest earlier today about Liv's intentions. Maybe everything is moving along exactly how it should be. For that to be the case, though, I have to follow through on the game plan. Find the strength, Christian, find the strength. But I can't end it yet, my curiosity is percolating. I need more answers.

"But Liv, I have to ask you something. You won't get mad, right?"

"Jesus, I'm not going to get mad, Christian. Just ask me."

"Well, I was in Tim's office today and I saw a picture of you and a young girl. Who is that?"

I can tell this strikes a chord, Liv's eyes instantly begin to swell, and her cheeks turn ruby red. She barely gets out her words. "That's my daughter," she says.

Honestly, I'm not shocked by this revelation. It's something I expected, but her emotion is what surprises me. "Liv, are you okay?" I ask.

She rests her spoon into the ice cream, places her hands over her eyes, she is trying to hold back the tears. I sit there, not knowing what to say or how to respond. After a short while, a tear drops from her right eye. She tries to regain her composure, gasps for air, but more tears come tumbling out.

I go to the counter, grab a few napkins, and give them to Liv. She twists them, dabs her eyes, and then fiddles with the napkin in her hands. "It's not what you think," she says.

I try to comfort her by reaching across the small table and taking each hand into mine. She looks me in the eyes while biting her upper lip to slow the waterworks. "I didn't expect to get into all of this."

"I'm sorry. I just . . . I just . . . I had to ask."

Liv cuts me off before I can get anything out. "I get it, Christian," she says. "You don't have to explain yourself. Why wouldn't you ask? You know."

I'm still bewildered at why it's such an ordeal. I mean, I understand the kid changes the dynamic, but the emotional rollercoaster is throwing me for a bit of a loop. "What is it, Liv?" I ask. "Are you okay?"

"I just need to catch my breath," she says. "Gimme a second."

She removes her right hand from mine, leaves her left in place, grabs the napkin, and starts dabbing her eyes again. Now, I'm starting to get nervous. What could it be?

"Three years ago, Tim and I were coming home from dinner in Manhattan. That night Chloe, our daughter, was staying at a friend's house in Armonk. She was six. It was midnight when we arrived to pick her up and she was already asleep. Tim plopped her in her booster seat, and she was sleeping again within seconds. We decided to take the backroads home that night."

Liv takes a minute to regroup. I have a feeling where this might be going, and I don't like it. I can tell from her drawn-out expression whatever she is about to tell me is much worse than the unease I'm experiencing.

"On the ride back, we got T-boned by a drunk driver running a red light and Chloe died."

I nearly knock over the milkshake as she says it. Now it's my eyes that feel swollen, probably where all the blood went from my stopped heart. I feel terrible, not only for Liv, but Tim too. I had no idea and I don't think anyone in the office knows, either. Why would we? It's not exactly the easiest thing to announce. "Hey, I'm your new boss. By the way, my six-year-old daughter died a couple years ago." Just doesn't make sense.

I sit here in front of a daughterless Mother, in disbelief, thinking no parent should have to witness their son or daughter die, let alone at the expense of some drunk in a pick-up truck. The pain running through her body must feel like a sledgehammer to the heart. All I can do is mutter, "That's awful. I'm so sorry, Liv."

We sit there for the next few minutes in complete silence. I slurp my milkshake and Liv eats her sundae slow bite after slow bite. It is the longest five minutes of my life. I am speechless. Sure, there is so much to still talk about, the trip is looming, but I don't want to make it more difficult so I stop asking questions. Liv breaks the ice.

"Christian, I'm happy I got this off my chest. Just reliving the moment over and over gets tiring, but it's part of my story now. Tim's too."

"You must really miss her," I say

"You have no idea. I'm always playing back in my mind what we could have done differently," she says. "Got a sitter that night? Taken the highway home? Not gone to dinner in the city with Tim's stupid friends? The possibilities are endless."

"You can't think about what could have been. That's going to kill you forever. The loss is hard enough."

"You're right. It's just so hard," she says.

I try to bring a little light into the darkness. I grab her hands and tell her, "You're a beautiful woman with at least another 40 years in front of you. Your future is bright."

"Forty years?" She asks.

"How old do you want to be? Anything after 80 is a blessing!"

"Okay, I can live with 40. You know, Tim and I really hit a rough patch for about a year after Chloe passed. Tim was doing well at work, I was home alone, and the thought of having another kid was starting to fade. We were just too hurt," she says. "Tim had amassed a bunch of company stock over the years, after Chloe passed he decided to sell it, and buy that Golden Beach house. It was our chance to escape and bring some joy back into our life and start over."

It made sense to me. They were scraping, crawling, and searching for anything to distract them from what happened. A living hell, I guess. I can only sit there, listening to her.

"It worked for a while too," she says. "For the first year after we bought the house, we went down every chance we had. We made some new friends. It was great. Year two, Tim took the new job with Perkins and we didn't go down as much. So, it didn't surprise me when he said he wanted to host the winner of that award down there. Just another way to get some use out of it."

"*That* award?" I say.

I see a hint of a smile from her. "Sorry, you know what I mean," she says. "Anyway, I go down there with Emma as often as I can just to get away. You remember Emma, right?"

"Yes, of course, the night we met she ran off with some guy dressed head to toe in John Varvatos."

Liv thought about it for a second and giggles. Finally, she's smiling again. "Right!" she says. "Wow—funny how everything seems to connect. That's Ty and he's actually our neighbor in Florida. He's a real character. Emma met him in Florida, then he was up in the city for the weekend, they were texting, and she got him to drive up here."

"Seems to connect alright!" I say, "John Varvatos saw us together. He's your neighbor which means he knows Tim."

"First of all, relax. Second, his name is Ty and trust me, he doesn't care! Third, he's not an immediate neighbor, he just lives in the area."

"You're killing me," I say shaking my head. She continues laughing.

"Relax, Ty is the exact opposite of Tim. They don't exactly see eye-to-eye. Actually, Ty is more like you. He has that playfulness." Liv reaches out and grabs my chin from across the table. "Don't ever lose that playfulness," she says.

"I'm just hoping I don't lose my job!"

Liv's eyes light up. "You'll be fine. Trust me!"

I sigh, let those words soak in, and take another sip of my milkshake.

The whole time we've been sitting there not one soul has walked into the shop. The girls behind the counter are just chatting and fooling around on their cellphones. It seems like the entire world stopped for Liv and me. I am supposed to be discussing how we'll play out this whole situation between us. I have to end it. I know the stakes, but after she tells me about her daughter, I feel a much deeper connection. Her aura is pulling me in like the world's strongest magnet.

Before the forces get too strong, I have to blurt it out. "I hate to say this, but you know we have to end this, right?"

"I know," she says.

I was expecting a much grander response. Maybe some pushback, but I get nothing. A piece of me wants her to fight for me. Tell me: no way, we can't stop, but she is too exposed to the harsh realities of life. I can understand, but still I'm hoping for a little push 'n' pull.

"God forbid something happens, like Tim does find out, then we can always fall back on we had no idea who each other were when we slept together," I say, then pause. "You know what I mean, right?"

"I do, but that back-up story seems better for you than it does for me. Think about it? You're in the clear because you just slept with a nice piece of ass," she says using air quotes. "You had no idea, it's easy to explain. However, me, I'm the whore who cheated on my husband with some random guy she knew nothing about."

"Right, but I'm the one with my life on the line."

"My life isn't?" She says.

"Okay. Ah, that came out wrong. You know what I mean?"

"Here's how I see it," Liv says. "The only way for us to have an equal amount of skin in the game is for us to sleep with each other again tonight."

Every organ in my body knows this is a bad idea, except my penis. The problem is: the penis is like a foreman. He bosses everyone around and the only way you get out of doing what he says is to quit the job. It's a love-hate relationship. The foreman gets the job done, but you're powerless.

Liv continues, "If this is going to be the last time we ever spend a night together, then we should probably take advantage of it."

Now, my personal foreman starts to rally my heart— the last time ever! It sounds so final. That's what I want, but why do I feel sad about it? I really do want her. Every part of her. That is something I can't deny. The penis and heart tandem is too much for my brain to handle. Shit.

"Fine, but here's the deal," I say and pause for a second.

"I'm listening," she says.

"You have to tell Tim you're not going to Golden Beach."

"No way," she says. "That will never fly. He'll freak out if I don't go with him. How about *you* don't go instead?"

"No way. I can't do that. It's an honor for me. Plus, Undercuffler will be there. I can't let him go alone. I can't let him get the upper hand. It will make me look bad."

"Christian!" she says, grabbing my chin again and looking me dead in the eye. "This is silly. Tim isn't going to find out. We're overthinking this. We're adults. It's just three nights and four days. It will come and go, and then it will be over."

I catch my breath. "You're right, you're right. We can handle it."

She takes her hand off my chin and sits back. "So, are you bringing a date?"

I knew this question was coming. I wanted to say, "Yeah, a piece of ass so hot that even you'd want to go down on her." But fuck, I have to tell her the truth.

"I'm bringing Jack."

"Jack?"

"Remember, my buddy from the other night?"

She almost spits out her ice cream. "You're bringing Jack? What?" She starts to laugh.

"What do you want from me!? I got no other options. Tim suggested it!"

"Like I said, *playful*. Only a playful guy would bring a good friend over a date to a work vacation."

"Whatever," I say dismissing it. But maybe she is onto something. I don't know. Either way, Jack is coming. I should just tell her what Tim said about "no whores," but the last thing I need is to stoke that fire.

I look over at her, peer directly into her eyes, and ask, "So are we really going to do this one last time then?"

"I think so," she says.

"Yeah?"

"Well, I want you," she says. "Do you want me?"

I nod and say, "My place."

"Let's go."

———

I don't have much to offer at my place except myself and alcohol, although tonight I'm pretty sure Liv will be okay with that.

I've got an empty fridge, minimal decor, few books scattered around, a guitar, big-screen TV in the living room, laptop, and four or five bottles of alcohol. Oh, and I keep some lemon-flavored club soda in the icebox for a makeshift Tom Collins.

The ride up the elevator is less eventful than last weekend. This time, fireworks are going off in my stomach. All nerves, no calm.

When we get inside, Liv takes her overcoat and bomber jacket off and tosses her stuff on the coffee table. She sits on the edge of the couch with her knees poking out of her jeans.

"So, this is how bachelors live these days?"

"What's the matter—you don't remember?"

She smiles and says, "Oh, I remember. I had a look around last week. Obviously that didn't scare me off."

"You want a drink—vodka, gin, whiskey, or tequila?"

"Just the essentials, huh?"

By this time, I'm standing in the kitchen and laughing to myself. I raise my voice to say, "Go easy on me will ya. I'm an unattached male!"

She yells back, "I'll take whatever you're having."

I walk over from the kitchen carefully balancing a full Tom Collins in each hand and making sure they don't topple over. Liv is perched on the couch with her nipples poking out from her T-shirt tucked into the front of her worn denim. The thought of what lies underneath is enough to feel the warmth between my legs, it almost buckles my knees, and sends the drinks flying.

Liv points to the drink. "What is it?"

"Tom Collins, well, kind of." I hand her one and she takes a sip.

"Tastes like club soda and gin to me."

"Well, I'm missing some key ingredients so, like I said, kind of."

"So, it's gin and soda?" she asks.

"Lemon soda," I say. "It's missing sugar and lemon juice."

"It'll do for now."

I smirk. "Happy you approve."

"What?"

"Nothing, you just make me laugh."

Liv grins. "Well, I have that effect on people," she says. "So, do you have any music?"

"Do I have any music?" I say. "Is that a serious question?"

"Okay, let's *play* some music. But here's a question I don't think I've asked you yet . . . What's your favorite album?"

"Wow. That's tough," I reply. "I grew up in the era of the song. I mean, not totally, but streaming killed albums. Don't you think?"

She puts her index finger over her lips and crinkles her brows. "I guess you're right," she says. "I think you can always make a case that the 'hit song' was more important than the album. These days very few people know albums, they just know the hit songs. In a way, albums were probably always more important for the artist."

It's this kind of sensibility that tickles me deep in my core, an area most women can never get to, nothing physical can reach. "You might be right."

"My Mom and Dad grew up in the hippie generation," she says. "They were all about peace, love, and happiness. I think that really seeped into me and was why I made some of my early life choices, it was all I knew. Then, eventually, I just wanted to escape the lifestyle I grew up in, but the music never left me. How could it? It was magical."

As she is speaking, I can't wait to jump in. "You know, I always liked music, but I didn't really get into it until college. My folks weren't into it so much," I say. "College is when I picked up playing the guitar and gained more of an appreciation for 60s and 70s era rock 'n' roll. I really dove in at that point."

"I knew you loved that music era," she says. "We talked about it last weekend. Too drunk to remember?"

I just laugh.

I don't really forget; I just pretend like I do. How could I forget? Her interest in rock 'n' roll was one of the unexplainable qualities that had me dazzled all week.

"I remember, I remember. The Stones song 'Miss You' came on at the Fatty Duck. That was actually in the late 70s," I say. "Okay, here you go, talk about full circle. 'Miss You' is a great song, but sounds nothing like the rest of the *Some Girls* album. For example, I don't even know how 'Beast of Burden' and 'Miss You' are on the same album."

"Wait, so do you like the album or song better?" she asks.

"Song, for sure," I reply. "Actually, did you know that song was the result of Jagger spending a little too much time in Studio 54?"

"What song? 'Beast of Burden'?"

"No, 'Miss You'."

"I didn't know that! It doesn't surprise me," she says. "He was supposedly a freak back then. I would have sex with him."

"Who wouldn't have sex with Jagger? The guy oozes sex. Even I wouldn't think twice." She hits my leg and takes a sip of her drink.

"It's true," she says.

"Okay, Mrs. Album. What's your favorite?" I ask.

"Ah, I knew this was coming. There's one album that I love, everything about it. It's almost like the soundtrack of my life."

"I'm on pins and needles. What is it?"

"*Imagine.*"

"Lennon? By himself, really? All those great Beatles albums—*Rubber Soul, Sgt. Pepper's, Abbey Road*—and Lennon by himself trumps them all?"

She stares at me. Her smile goes flat. Her eyes turn sullen. "Christian," she says. "Those are all great albums, but *Imagine* is special for a different reason. Hear me out . . ."

I take down half of my drink in one gulp waiting for her response.

Liv continues, "That album was about passion, honesty, and stood for something bigger. You had everything that was going on with the civil rights movement and Vietnam. Lennon was an enormous star. Yet he found himself under duress for leaving the Beatles. Or—should I say—for the idea that Yoko drove him away from the Beatles. Really, he was just a guy who fell in love. Was Yoko nuts? Maybe. So what? It was Lennon saying, 'This is who I am. This is what I stand for. Take it or leave it.'"

"Wait—so I still haven't heard you say anything about the actual album?"

"Don't be a wiseass," she says. "I love *everything* about that album. You have 'Imagine,' the song, as powerful and collective as any song could ever be, one of the greatest songs ever. And songs that ring so true to the human condition, 'Crippled Inside' and 'How.' John literally says *screw you* to Paul with 'How Do You Sleep?' Some people don't like that, but I think it's the perfect embodiment of how there's darkness and pain within all of us. A little voice fighting to be heard. I'm not going to go through every song, but I can if you want me to."

Right as I begin to answer, she jumps back in. "Oh, and you have to love how the album ends. 'Oh Yoko!' is just this upbeat jingle that leaves you feeling good, which is needed after going through such a gambit of human emotions. It just pulls everything together. Kind of like: *here it is, she's my future*. The whole thing, it's just a very emotionally charged album. One that I've gone back to so many times throughout my life."

I can see her spirit shooting out from every orifice of her body. I can feel how much she really loves this album. She almost has me convinced, enough so that I put the album on and for the next 40 minutes we sit, drinking our cocktails, and listening to it straight through. Maybe this is an early look at heaven. God, I hope I make it. Liv talks me through each track. Her insights all relate to the highs and lows of her life. I can't figure out whether I'm more enamored with her physical or mental being. It is her beauty that grips me, but her inner child that holds me. The tiger in front of me has been caged for too long, domesticated and tamed, and this makes me sad. Not just for her, but for us. This all feels more like the beginning rather than the end.

Just as she interprets, the album ends on a high note. The alcohol swirls in our bellies, and she asks me to play her a song on my Little Martin. This always happens: alcohol plus guitar equals song.

"Ah, do I have to?"

"Yes, you have to!"

"Ugh, fine," I say. The guitar represents everything I wish I was in this world. Maybe this is why I always cringe to play in front of people. Everyone wants to hear you, but nobody really listens. It also represents a rough time in my life after I stopped playing baseball, the guitar is where my time went, and my Dad hated that. Well, there, and drinking and chasing women. "What do you want me to play?"

"Anything," she says.

I hate when people say, "anything," it's like: what the eff do I play? There's too many songs to choose from. I fire through songs in my head, but I can't think of anything. Plus, the gin has me a little foggy.

"Do I really have to?" I ask.

"Fine," she says. "You don't *have* to."

Shit, I can't go down like that. I have to play at least one song. "No, no I will. I want to," I say.

I've got to pick a song that will tug on the heartstrings. One that doesn't matter if I am bad or not. Hurry, Christian, think. Somewhere deep in the crevices of my mind, I find my inner salesman. Corny, probably, but perfect for two star-crossed lushes drowning in emotion at midnight.

I strum an acoustic version of 'Something Like Olivia' by John Mayer.

Her smile deepens and there's a twinkle in her eye. The rhythm only has the faintest resemblance to the original, but the lyrics seem to put her in a daze more powerful than five Tom Collins drinks. Certainly, enough to distract her from the fact that I'm not John Mayer.

I finish the song and she whispers, "About me?"

I smile. "Did you like it?"

"How could I not?" she says, smiling. "It gave me chills."

"I guess that's a good thing."

"Christian. You're *so* good," she says. "Wow. I am impressed . . . and flattered." Liv flips her hair over one eye and continues, "You know, you didn't have to play that song to have me tonight, right?"

Music has a way of reducing people down to their purest form. I bet she's wondering if I mean what I just sang, but she didn't ask, it doesn't matter. That's the power of music. I place the guitar on the ground and look at her, saying everything I want to say with my eyes.

Liv sits there looking back at me, our eyes locked, saying a million things without using a word. The temperature is rising. She slowly stands up and begins walking toward the bedroom. I'm hypnotized: her bare feet tiptoeing along on the hardwood floor and her slim body swaying from side to side are mesmerizing. At the doorway of the bedroom, she removes her T-shirt in slow motion and lets it fall to the floor. Standing there in nothing but her jeans with her bare back facing me, she looks over her left shoulder and pauses for the slightest moment. "Are you coming or what?" she says.

Her clothes sprinkled all over my living room remind me of the scattered thoughts I had about our predicament. But her body is a glowing light pole in the night. Just leading me further into the abyss. Her perfect shoulders only accentuated by the plushness and tone of her skin leaves me no choice but to gulp once then run to her.

She scampers into the bedroom and, when I walk in, she's lying there completely naked. I want to be romantic, but an eroticism overwhelms me. It's not just my mental being that is under a spell. I can feel the physical nature of her presence brewing under my jeans. The only thing that surpasses the thought of my lips on her stomach is my lips on her stomach.

With each kiss down her midsection, I feel her legs tighten. There's a peach fuzz that you can only see from the angle I am at, but can feel on my mouth. It's the feeling of enchantment. Little kiss by little kiss. I can hear the sound of her heart. I roll my eyes up and she is looking down at me. A paparazzi to the experience, her brows furrow and eyes squint, portraying a bright tone of green.

She can't take it anymore. Liv leans up, tosses my head

back, tears off my shirt, and pulls me closer to her. She throws me to the side, kisses my stomach, and unbuttons my jeans. The only thing that lies between the truth is a thin piece of denim. Certainly, not enough to stop the inevitable. A tingling sensation runs through me and I lose feeling in my penis for a brief moment. It's the goose-bumps that remind me this isn't a dream. Life isn't being sucked out of me, it's being blown into me. Full of energy and completely attuned, I am merciless with her for the rest of the night. How can I not be?

It is everything I wanted and now have, even if it is only for one night.

TEN

THE TWO WEEKS LEADING UP to the trip are torture. I dodge Tim like an ex-girlfriend in a bar. At every sighting, I turn the other way. I barely reply to his emails, give short responses, and avoid any unnecessary interactions. I just don't want the reminder of Liv in my mind, and I know way more than I should about Tim, the Father and husband. It is a mindfuck of epic proportions. I keep telling myself, "I can do anything for four days, right?" I'm not sure how much I believe it, but it's all I got.

I follow through with my end of the bargain and quit Liv cold turkey. I get off pretty easily and, really, I have no choice. I don't know where she lives, I don't have her phone number, and I'm not searching to find out. I'd be lying if I don't say each day that I hope she breaks her commitment to me. She knows where I live. I could come home one day and see her standing there, waiting in the lobby of my apartment building.

One night I even had a dream that she was there, and I woke up in a cold sweat then couldn't fall back asleep.

Hate when that happens. I had an important meeting the next morning and I felt like a zombie. It was brutal.

As the trip inches closer, I get more and more one- or two-line emails from Tim. Emails like, "You all set to go have some fun in Florida?"

It's all standard, although I can't escape the thought in my mind that one of those emails will be the one that drops the hammer. Is it a thought I'm going to have to learn to live with forever? I don't know, but it sure feels like it.

Finally, the day arrives to fly down to Florida. It's a wet day and I don't like flying in the rain. There's more turbulence. I'm usually good with flying, but the take off is the worst part. Your body can't adjust fast enough to changes in altitude. Never mind when the weather is bad, then the jet bounces up and down and you lose your stomach about three or four times. The entire time I ask myself, "How necessary is this trip?" That's my greatest fear, dying in a plane crash on a trip I didn't have to go on, what a terrible way to go. This one is necessary. Dangerous, but necessary. For work, but also to see Liv. It might be the last time I see her.

The sweetest words are, "We've reached cruising altitude. It's now safe to unbuckle your seatbelts." I love those words. The flight flattens out and you get your stomach back for a while.

Jack and I don't talk much until the day we meet at the airport. He's busy, I'm busy, I don't know, but we just haven't seen each other much. He does know about the new developments in my situation, though. I gave him an abbreviated version of the story: Liv and I ended it, but we slept with each other again. He doesn't need to know about the emotion or connection involved, most guys don't seem to want to hear about that stuff anyway. The truth is:

being feminine is too big of a shot to the ego. It's dumb, but I play by the rules. Jack doesn't need to know any more, anyway.

Last weekend, I played hooky from going out with Jack while suffering from Liv withdrawals. Just couldn't get myself to go boozing, but saying you can't go out because you miss a girl too much just don't fly. Maybe in the movies that's endearing. In the real world, your buddies look at you like you've been in an institution or something. A good catch is the best remedy for being lovesick, but that means I have to go fishing. I'm not crazy, I just don't have the spirit I need to entertain other women. I can't bring myself to go fishing. Not yet. Somewhere in the back of my mind, I'm hoping something strange will happen that will enable Liv and I to be together. It's my little fantasy. I don't even know if she wants that, but it doesn't stop me from thinking about it, even when I know it's only a pipe dream. Maybe that's why I can't stop thinking about it. It's kind of like playing the lottery, despite the crappy odds there's an imprint in my mind that will forever read, *Maybe*.

It's a full flight. I'm sitting in the window seat, Jack in the middle, and a little old lady on the aisle. If there's one thing Jack respects, it's the pull of a woman, so he doesn't break my balls about sleeping with Liv again. Not too bad, anyway.

"So, you banged her again, huh?" he says.

"So, I banged her again," I say. We both chuckle.

"What are you going to do if she tries to pull a move on you down there?" he asks.

"Not a chance that's going to happen," I say. "Her husband, my boss, is going to be there."

"Yeah, but what if?" he says. "I mean, we're in the same house, dude. There's going to be alcohol. It's Florida, it's hot, people show more skin in the heat."

I look at him, and say, "People show more skin in the heat?"

Jack laughs. "What? They do!"

"You're ridiculous," I say and shake my head. "Anyway, I'll tell her to kick rocks."

"I'm not too sure about that."

"It's a moot point anyway," I say. "She's not a dumbass. She knows the situation. We all do."

"*And* if I had a dollar every time I heard that one, I'd be a rich man," Jack says then adjusts himself in the seat. "So, what's the deal with this trip?"

"What do you mean?"

"Well, you know . . . " he says. "As much as it's a vacay, it's also a work trip. You're going to be with your boss and co-worker. So, are there going to be, like, planned things to do? Are we going to be able to cut out at night? Like, what's the deal?"

I press that little round button, move the seat back, and respond. "Right. Right. So, there's no *specific* work events. As far as I know, we're just going to be enjoying South Florida," I say. "I mean, the house is in a pretty sweet location. I'm sure Tim has some shit planned, but nothing stuffy. Usually bosses like to show their human side in these non-work atmospheres. It's like the corporate-y way to say, 'I'm a cool guy, too. I just have to be different at work.' You know, get the employees and their wives on their side."

The flight attendant approaches. "Would you like something to drink? We also have peanuts, cookies, or pretzels. Would you like anything?" she asks.

"I'll have peanuts and a club soda," I tell her.

"Yeah. I'll have what he's having," Jack says then looks at me. "So, what were you saying?"

"Didn't you hear me? I'm not going to repeat the whole spiel. Basically, I'm sure it's just going to be fun."

Jack takes our stuff from the flight attendant, hands me my goodies, and takes a sip of his club soda. "Ahhhh," he says with a sigh. "It's a little weird that I'm coming, no?"

"You're just thinking about that now?" I say. "We have already been over this!" We both laugh.

"Maybe a little strange, but it's fine," I continue. "I think, in a weird way, Tim likes that I'm bringing you."

"Hm. We're definitely hitting Miami, right? Like, we're not just going to be cooped up in the house, right?"

"Golden Beach is, like, smack between Fort Lauderdale and Miami. We'll play it by ear, but you know how things go once people start drinking."

He sits back in the seat. "Yeah, everyone is up for everything."

"Exactly," I say. "It'll be fine."

Jack puts his hat over his eyes and falls asleep.

I've never been one to sleep on a plane. On the way, I'm too busy thinking about wherever I'm going. Maybe on the way home, once everything is over and nothing to be excited about, then I can sleep.

With Jack asleep, I have time to think about Golden Beach. I've driven through it before, but never stopped there. No reason, really. It's all residential, most are multi-million-dollar properties, it might be the smallest town in Florida. It rests on the edge of Miami-Dade County, the last stop before you enter Broward County.

It's sort of a crap shoot which airport you fly into—Fort Lauderdale or Miami International. Just another thing to get nervous about. What if I fly into the wrong airport today? Another tragic way to go, picking the wrong airport, talk about shit luck. Fucking planes. They always bring morbid thoughts to my mind. There's too much to think about with this trip. Liv, Tim, Undercuffler, my penis pointing me in the wrong direction. I need something to distract me.

I scroll through the movie selection but realize we only have about 90 minutes left on the flight. I can't start a movie and not finish it. That's just more torture and Lord knows I don't need any more of that. I open the window shade that has been closed since take off, crunch a few peanuts, and flip through the in-flight magazine. Nothing seems to engage me so I stare out the window some more. Is that the thought someone has right before they join the mile-high club? I don't really get the fascination with that, though. Gripping, certainly, but why not just wait until you land? Let the tension build up. The chase is usually the best part anyway. Does it count if you're on a private jet? I have more respect for the ones who pull it off on a commercial jet. The bathrooms are tiny, and, well, you're with 120 other people. Oh, I guess I can see it now, the value is in the difficulty.

My drifting is disrupted by a knock to my right elbow. I turn my head from the window and Jack is opening his eyes. "Hey dude. Is it hot in there?" he asks me.

I always travel with a hoodie and sweatpants. I never like to be chilly on an airplane, the travel anxiety is already bad enough, forget being cold and uncomfortable. I'm not hot at all. So, I reply, "No dude, I'm good."

He takes off his jacket, pulls down the neck of his hooded sweatshirt, and looks over at me with his eyes fully open. I ask, "Are you alright?"

"Yeah, I'm good. Just hot. Trying to get some air."

"You want some water?"

"Sure."

I hit the service button on the screen in front of me. It takes a minute or two and then the flight attendant comes over. "Can I have a couple bottles of water?" I ask.

"Couple?"

"Yeah. One for me and one for him."

Jack doesn't look terrible, so I'm not really worried or anything. He actually looks fine. She brings over the waters, Jack rips one from her hand, starts slugging it down before she can even hand mine to me. I apologize to her. "Sorry about that. Apparently he's thirsty."

"I can see that," she says. "It's fine."

"Are you alright?" I ask Jack again.

Jack takes a big gasp. "Much better now." But his eyes suggest otherwise, and his face seems a little flush. It looks more like he's trying to be much better now, than is much better.

I turn my head back to the window, not even five seconds pass, and I can feel Jack rustling next to me as he takes off his sweatshirt.

I look back. "Still hot?"

"Yeah. I'm just trying to get comfortable. Do you mind if I drink your water?" I don't even answer, and Jack grabs it off my tray table.

I notice a bead of sweat fall from his head. Something is definitely not right with this dude. He looks at me. "I need some air."

"Where are you going to get air? We are 30,000 feet in the sky," I say.

Okay, maybe that isn't the best response, sweat is now streaming down his forehead and his upper lip is shivering. What the heck?

He's trying to keep calm and not draw any attention from other people on the plane, but something is obviously wrong. Now he's in his T-shirt, two bottles of water deep, and panting like a dog at the beach, I hit the button again calling for the flight attendant.

"Just keep breathing, buddy," I say.

Jack's right arm bumps the lady next to him and her old eyes possess a look of concern and sadness. She asks me, "Is he alright?"

Why the fuck is she asking me? Relax, I've got to be nice, she's like 80.

"He's just hot," I tell her.

"He doesn't look alright." I know lady, just bear with us over here. Relax, be nice.

"He's alright," I say. "He just needs to get up and walk around. Can you get up so he can stand up?"

It takes her a moment to stand up in her creaky frame. Ah, poor lady. The flight attendant arrives before she even gets one leg in the aisle.

"What can I do for you?" the flight attendant asks. She sees Jack sweating profusely in only a T-shirt now.

"Is he alright?" she asks.

"I need some air. I need some air. That's it!"

The rest of the plane starts pointing, whispering, and chatting. Who's the wreck in seat 19B?

The flight attendant asks, "Did you take anything before you got on the plane?"

"No," Jack replies.

"Are you sure?"

"Yes. I'm freaking sure. I need some air!"

"Okay, okay," the flight attendant says. Then she reaches over the old lady, grabs Jack's hand to help him up. Jack tries to squeeze by and steps on the little lady's foot.

"Oh my," she yelps. Can this get any more ridiculous? Be nice, I tell myself, she's old. Jack makes it through and walks to the back of the plane drenched in his sweat.

"Are you okay?" I ask the lady.

"Thanks, young fellow," she says looking up at me. "I'm okay. Is he alright?"

"Geez, I hope so."

I sit back down and space out for a couple of minutes, then look back over my seat. Jack is sitting in the flight attendant area with an oxygen mask over his nose and mouth. He looks a little better, but it's hard to tell. I want to go back and see him, but I figure it's best to give him some space. Ten minutes go by and I can't resist pressing the service button again. When the flight attendant comes down the aisle, I ask how he is doing.

"He's fine, we think he just had an onset of anxiety."

"Like a panic attack?"

"Oh, I used to get those," the little old lady says. Why is she talking?

"Yes, something like that," the flight attendant says. "Sometimes people get claustrophobic on the plane and it triggers a rush of anxiety. Good news is that he's not sweating anymore, he's calm, and doing well."

"That's great. Thank you," I say and reach out to shake her hand.

"Of course," she says. Then continues, "You can go back and see him, if you'd like."

On the way back, I gaze into a few people's eyes, some look worried and others look tired. It only takes about 30 seconds to get back there.

"Jack, you alright buddy?"

"Yeah man. I'm good. I told you I just needed some air."

"Right," I say, then smirk. "You just needed some air."

"I'm going to sit back here until we're ready to land," he says.

"No problem. This ever happen before?"

"Sometimes I get mild anxiety, but never on an airplane before. I don't even know how it happened. Just started getting hot, felt boxed in, and next thing I know I'm gasping for air."

"Well, you're good now?"

"Next stop. Sunny Florida," he says.

I walk back to my seat, maneuver around the little old lady to avoid any more catastrophes, and plop myself down. "Your friend okay?" she asks.

I nod.

I hear her say under her breath, "Everyone is dealing with something."

She's right. I never knew Jack dealt with anxiety. I mean, things always seem to roll right off his back. I meditate on that idea for a moment, but the stillness and any empathy quickly start to fade. Is this a sign of things to come? I don't need any more damn obstacles.

I look back over my right shoulder, Jack's laughing and smiling with the flight attendant. Fuckin' Jack.

ELEVEN

THE DRIVE DOWN A1A in South Florida is unmistakable. It's lined with palm trees and sky-high buildings. The Atlantic Ocean is to the east and the Intercoastal is tucked one block or two inland on the west.

For the entire Uber ride from the airport to the house, I don't let Jack live down his airplane episode. Sure, I'm being an asshole, but this is what we do. Ultimately, I'm the one who's really screwed, anyway. He doesn't let me forget that either. Every chance he gets, he gives it back to me.

"So how is this trip going to end? You fired standing there with a rubber hanging from your Johnson," he says.

"Real funny! Dumb-ass."

"Don't worry," he says. "I'll drag your ass into Miami and we'll find you someone to occupy that mushy heart of yours." We both laugh, gaze out the window, and take in the sun-soaked scenery that surrounds us.

He is right, though. I can't wait to see Liv. Oddly, I want to see how she is going to act. I know how she is when she's with me, but I'm curious about how she will act in front of Tim and around all of us. I should probably be worrying a little more about myself, but thinking about her is more fun. I have countless images of her forged in my memory. Her eating ice cream, listening to music, those seductive eyes looking straight through me, all the while her moaning plays in the background.

You know you've hit Golden Beach when the apartment and condo buildings turn to residential homes on both sides. The entire town can't be more than a mile long separated by A1A. The east is nothing but beachfront homes, while the west is partly mainland and three small islands—North, Central, and South. Tim's house is nestled on a cul-de-sac at the southern tip of Central Island. Only about a thousand people call Golden Beach home, hard to even think of it as a town, nonetheless it is.

The sun is blistering when we pull up to the house around 2.30pm.

"Looks small," Jack says.

He's right, it doesn't look like much from the street. Well-maintained, but not too big. A paver driveway edged with green grass and palm trees on either side leads up to a one-car garage on the left and faces toward the next-door neighbor to the right. A black, two-door Jeep Wrangler is parked in the driveway. Set back to the right is an arched double-door entrance to a bleach-white house. Very Florida. It has a funky roof with a long, slanted pitch running from right to left. It gives the house this modern-architectural feel—odd but cool.

The house sits right on the Intercoastal, the waterway that runs down the South Florida coast and divides the mainland from Golden Beach. "I got a feeling the house is going to open up in the back," I tell Jack.

I tip the cabbie, grab our bags, walk to the house, and ping the doorbell. Will Liv open it? Just as the thought enters, Tim opens the door. "Christian! You made it," he says. "And this is your friend?"

I shake Tim's hand and introduce him to Jack. They chitchat for a moment as we step into the house. Tim suggests giving us a quick tour.

"Can I have a drink first?" I ask.

He laughs, thinking I'm joking, but I'm serious. Ah, whatever, I don't need one yet. Tim shows us around.

The house has a completely open floor plan, living room, kitchen, bar and dining areas all seem to flow together. You can see straight through to the back of the house where floor-to-ceiling windows give a view to the backyard.

Everything is white—floors, furniture, and walls. The interior matches the exterior, it's all very modern. There's an open staircase that leads to a one-floor master suite equipped with a bedroom, office, walk-in closet, and fully outfitted bathroom that makes most bedrooms look small. Off the master, there's a huge balcony that has a 180° view that overlooks the in-ground pool, boating dock, and Inter-coastal waterway.

We make our way back downstairs and Tim shows us to the guest bedrooms. There's three in total. A big one on the right side of the home with its own bath and double doors that open to the pool. Undercuffler and Molly are staying in that room. The other two bedrooms flank the house to the left, but only one has sliders out to the pool. I'm staying in that room. Jack is staying in the other bedroom which faces the front side of the house. It's a little room with one window that looks out toward the driveway. There's a full bathroom in the hallway that Jack and I have to share.

"Of course, I get the little kid's bedroom," Jack says.

"Oh relax, it's just small," I say. "It's not decorated in dinosaurs."

"I'm kidding, geez," he says.

"I know, I know."

All three of us move into the kitchen and congregate around the center island.

I ask Tim, "When is Undercuffler arriving?"

"Not sure. I suspect he'll be here soon," Tim says. "I'm happy you got in early, though. We'll go relax by the pool."

Jack says, "I'm going to go make a few calls, settle in until everyone else gets here, and take a nap."

"Yeah? You just got here," says Tim. He opens the fridge and starts pulling out beverages.

"I had a rough night last night and the flight was . . . uh, a bit rocky."

I laugh to myself. "Yeah. The flight was a bit rocky alright."

"Really?" Tim asks.

Jack and I look at each other. I sure as hell don't want to get into it right now. Maybe it would break the ice a bit, but I don't want Tim to think that I have a nervous wreck with me. Sounds shitty, but I'm trying to control the situation as much as possible.

Tim continues to take stuff out of the fridge. "Well, suit yourself. I hired a chef to make us dinner tonight," he says. "Be ready by 7pm."

"You got it," Jack says then looks over to me. "I'm going to owe you one after this trip."

"You will," Tim says while pointing at me. "But this guy right here, he deserves it. Who cares if he's got no bride?"

"Ooo, low blow, huh?" I say.

Jack heads off to his room. "What would you like to drink?" Tim asks.

"I'll take a Tom Collins."

"Ah, what's in that again?"

"Club soda, lemon juice, sugar, and gin."

"What happened to vodka soda or a beer?" Tim asks.

"You asked!" I say with a smile.

He rummages through the fridge then walks over to the small bar area. "I don't have anything except club soda," he says. "Who still drinks a Tom Collins?"

I laugh, but inside I'm thinking—me, asshole!

"Ah, just give me Corona and lime," I say. "Tell me you have a lime."

He laughs. "I got a lime."

I gotta admit, this all feels pretty normal. Tim is a regular boss and the trip is just something to honor me for my work. We are a couple guys just breaking balls in the kitchen, then the phone rings.

"Hey, baby," I hear Tim say.

How did I forget about Liv? I'm hoping that's her on the other line, otherwise Tim is a real asshole. Maybe I'm hoping for that, too.

"Right, right. Hey, can you pick up some gin and lemon juice?" he says.

"Sugar?" he asks. "Why would I need sugar?" Tim listens then responds, "No we're good."

Holy shit. Did Liv already slip up? And then have to recover with an excuse. He covers the phone with his left hand. "I got you," he says to me.

I mouth the word, "Thanks."

Liv knows what I drink, and she knows that I'm coming, that has to be her. Is she thinking about me?

"No, I know. It's not for me, honey. Christian and his butt buddy just arrived."

Oh, so he's got jokes. Please don't make this hard on

me, Tim. I can ruin you—and my life—right now. I mouth out the word, "Funny."

Tim smiles. "Okay, see you soon," he says then he hangs the phone up.

"Now you will be able to have your Tim Collins."

"*Tom* Collins, Tim, *Tom* Collins."

"Oh right," he says. "How can I forget?"

I shouldn't ask about who was on the phone, sugar, or anything that might raise red flags, but screw it. It's just one question.

"Who was that?" I ask.

"It was Olivia," Tim says. "She's out shopping with friends. She'll be back in a little bit."

"Great. I look forward to seeing her again." What the fuck? Why would I say that?

"Oh yeah? Forget Olivia, wait 'til you see her friends," Tim says. "Maybe they'll stick around, then you'll really be in luck."

"Oh, really?"

"Yeah, well, unless Jack is, ya know . . . good enough for you."

Why does he have all these damn jokes about being a homo or something? What's wrong with homos anyway? Just more costume humor of corporate America that's never tangled with the after-4am crowd. It's mostly harmless banter and I have no choice but to take it like a heavy bag, shot after shot. I did bring Jack, after all. Maybe Liv's friends will actually be hot. It'll feel awkward, but, shit, at least it'll provide me some relief.

"C'mon let's go out to the pool and try to get a few rays before everyone else gets here," Tim says. "There's actually something I want to talk to you about."

Talk about? He would have already 'talked' to me

about Liv, so I'm not worried about that. It feels more work-like to me.

I get changed and go lie down in a lounge chair beside the pool. Tim gets there a minute later, brings our beers over, and we watch the boats pass by on the Intercoastal for a while. We're both wearing sunglasses which is good because the sun is reflecting off the pool directly into our eyes. It's also good because it means your eyes can wander and you won't look like a creep.

Tim has the body of a 50-year-old man, not fat, not old, but 50. It's the kind of body a costume hides well. He's trying, but time catches up, and 50 is 50. Plus, when you have money, it grabs you and says, "C'mere and have a taste of the good life," and his body shows he's been listening to that voice.

We sit there making small talk about the weather and what not, then he lowers his glasses as if to get serious for a moment.

"Christian," he says. "I'm happy we got some time to chat before everyone else gets here."

These are normal words you might hear from a boss, but, in my situation, any moment can turn into the butcher block. I'm walking on a tightrope that could snap at any minute. I don't lower my sunglasses, afraid of what he might say, and I continue to look forward.

"Me too," I say. "What's up?"

"Your work has been exemplary Christian, since I've been at Perkins, and, from what I understand, prior to that too. I've seen the year-over-year numbers, and I want you to hear this from me."

I wiggle the lime in the near empty Corona bottle and listen intently to hear what's coming next.

"Nobody else knows this, but Olson is going to be

moving on to a new role in the company. He's actually relo-
cating. I want you to be his replacement. I see a lot of me in
you, Christian." Damn, I hate when he says that, but holy
shit. This isn't just another pat on the ass, go get 'em Char-
lie, here's some more praise. Is he really promoting me?

"Nobody else knows about this, and I'd like to keep it
quiet for now. Mostly out of respect for Olson. His move
will be official in a month and it will be announced in a
couple weeks, at which time I'd like to have a replacement
to announce along with it. You're the one, Christian.
You're my guy." I can tell he's looking at me. I don't move,
I just sit there, soaking in everything I've just heard.

"So, what do you think?" he asks after a few seconds.

"I think I'll have another beer," I say.

Tim laughs and says, "Look, I know it's going to be a
lot more responsibility, but with that comes a raise. Big one.
Actually, a completely different comp plan with stock
options and bonuses."

"Wow. I don't really know what to say, Tim," I say.
"Coming down here, I did not anticipate this."

"Honestly, neither did I," he says. "But then the whole
thing happened with Olson last week. I thought, well, I
have two of my best coming down to Florida in a week
and I did tell you before the awards dinner you had my
vote. After a closer look at everything, you *still* have my
vote."

"It's really an honor that you would consider . . . "

Tim cuts me off. "Before you say anything, I know it's a
lot to take in. It's a different role for you. I'm not expecting
you to jump in my lap. Although, I wouldn't mind." He
laughs, then continues. "So, take a week or so and think it
over. Then let me know. I don't want to talk about it
anymore. Let's just enjoy the weekend."

I take a deep breath, knowing he fully expects me to

take the role. "Take some time to think it over" is the standard mumbo jumbo.

"Deal," I say.

Tim takes the final swig of his beer, throws his arms out as the sun beats on his chest, and lets out a big, "Ahhh! Look at this," he says. "Paradise. You're on your way kid."

I smile and he continues, "Plus, you'll get to work a lot more with me." He raises his empty bottle to salute, so I raise mine.

"Let me grab you another," he says.

Out of everything Tim just told me, it's those last couple sentences that are still lingering in my mind. I'd have to see a lot more of him? Now, how the fuck was I going to manage doing that? An entire relationship built on a lie? Is it even possible? I guess people do it all the time, but I can't imagine it ending well. Does it ever? Maybe I can manage to get five or ten good years in before it all burns down. Maybe Tim will get fired at some point. Anything can happen, I guess.

As I'm about to dive deeper into the thought, I'm distracted by Tim's voice talking to someone in the kitchen. I turn, lower my shades, and spot Undercuffler and Molly.

Tim points out to me and I raise my hand up. They wave back. Undercuffler begins to walk over.

"Hey buddy," I say.

"Not much different from the office, huh?" he says. "You're working extra hard over here?" Typical dumb Undercuffler joke. I stand up and shake his hand.

"Something like that," I say. "Glad to see you made it down okay."

"Yes, it was a rough morning," he says. "We had some problems with the little one and Molly's Mom had something come up so she couldn't watch her for the weekend. I had to get a hold of my Mother. She was kind of complaining. But we made it."

"Sounds like fun."

"Ha, yep, fun," he says. "I'm just looking forward to a few days of relaxation."

"I hear ya, man."

Tim comes waltzing over and hands me another beer. "Mark, let me show you around."

There's something about knowing you have one up on a guy that just makes you feel good. It's a shitty thing to think, but it's true. Just knowing Tim prefers me over Undercuffler helps me act differently toward him. There's no pressure, no competition anxiety, just confidence. The idea of me being Undercuffler's boss starts to get me hard, not that I'd be a total asshole, but it would be nice. I consider the alternative and instantly feel my bowels move. Fuck that. The thought of Undercuffler as my boss makes me queasy. Maybe it wouldn't be much different from the double team I get from him and Olson now. Ah, whatever. I don't need to worry about that today. I sit back down, put my feet up, and intend to enjoy what's left of this sunny afternoon, but even that gets ruined. Within ten minutes, I feel a drop of rain. I open my eyes to see mostly sun with a patch of dark clouds coming from the southeast. I hear Tim yell from the kitchen, "Come on inside!"

The rain starts to pick up, I grab my shit, and lightly jog back to the house. "That sucks, huh?" I say as I walk through the sliding doors, closing them behind me. I stamp my wet feet on the mat.

"It's not so bad," Tim says. "Just your typical Florida afternoon sun shower. They come and go."

The water starts to come down in droves, you can hear the raindrops pelt the windows.

Tim continues, "Don't worry. It'll pass."

Undercuffler tells Tim about his busy morning, Molly is in their room unpacking, and after a few minutes he joins her to rest up until dinner. Tim and I stand there in the kitchen, watching the water running down the windows. It resembles a melting face, maybe a sad one, reminding you that it was nothing but sunny minutes earlier.

"What time is dinner again?" I ask Tim.

"7pm. The chef should be getting here shortly."

I looked at my watch. I have about two hours. "I'm going to head to my room for a while."

"Sounds good. See you in a few."

As soon as I lay my head on the pillow, I hear a person come through the front door and some faint conversation. Is that Liv? I'm too exhausted to get up or to listen any closer, but a sixth sense tells me that might be her.

TWELVE

I OVERSLEEP, which makes me slightly late to dinner. I feel bad because Jack doesn't know anybody except Liv, who he is not supposed to know. This is the thought that puts a fire under my ass. I can hear soft banter in the background suggesting people are mingling about in the main room. Sometimes having no time to think about what to wear and how you look is better than having too much time. No second guessing. What's it matter, anyway? Within minutes I'll be thrown into the tornado, spun in any direction, just hoping I land on my feet.

I don't walk more than two steps into the main room before I hear my name howled out, "Christian. You're alive!" It's Jack and he's in the kitchen with Undercuffler and Tim. They're fixing some drinks while the chef runs around with a helper plating appetizers. Jack appears to be in a particularly good mood.

I ask him, "How many drinks have you had already?"

He smiles. "Only two!"

"I've got your drink waiting for you." Tim yells to me.

Undercuffler blurts out, "You've got quite the friend here!"

I'm assuming he's referring to Jack. Undercuffler is a stiff, so the range of things Jack could have said or done is too wide to even guess. I'm left to only speculate. I notice Tim is making four martinis. That's Liv's drink. Where is she? It seems like two too many, though, until I see four heads with long hair through the sliders. Unless I'm delusional, there are definitely four females sitting on the patio furniture.

"Everyone's outside, let's go," Tim says. "Christian, I have a couple friends I want to introduce you to."

"You're going to like this," Jack says.

It's a beautiful evening. The rain has subsided, only leaving the slightest breeze. The back patio looks different in the dark, it's lined with tiki torches flickering in the night sky and reflecting off the pool water. It makes for a calming effect, which I'm going to need to get through the night. There is yacht rock playing on the stereo system. I can't make out the song, but that's probably a good thing, palatable ones in this genre are few and far between.

The first time I saw Liv at the Fatty Duck, she was eating dinner with her back to me, and that's exactly how I'm greeted now. That dirty blonde hair and those shoulders are a dead giveaway. Sure enough, there's two other females sitting on the couch, also with their backs to me as I walk out. The only one facing me is Molly with her girlish grin and rosy cheeks.

"Liana and Emma, meet Christian," says Tim.

Motherfucker Emma is here, too. I have to pretend like it's my first time meeting her. She doesn't slip up, either. I must admit, Emma looks quite different under the Miami sky than she did in CT. More relaxed. Liana is very alluring with long, straight black hair, tan skin, and large breasts. No question about it, they're fake, she seems to possess a confidence that radiates off her. It is her youthfulness that sticks out amongst all traits, though. Not overly young, just noticeable by comparison.

"Pleasure to meet you both," I say and shake their hands.

All the women are wearing sundresses and heels, not leaving much to the imagination with their sun-kissed necks, shoulders, and legs all exposed. Even Molly, who apparently has left her homeliness back north, isn't too shabby.

Tim points at Liv and says, "And you remember my wife, Olivia?"

The words come out of his mouth in slow motion, Liv gives me a quick glance, the first time we've crossed eyes in over two weeks, then takes a sip of her martini.

I stutter for a moment, brace myself, then sputter out, "Of course. How can I forget? Pleasure to see you, Liv."

Fuck. Did I just say that? Yup, I did. Tim furrows his brow and says, "Liv!? Nobody has called you that in years."

Jack butts in, "He always calls people by their nicknames. For instance, my real name is Jackson." I can't figure out what's worse: me slipping with Liv or Jack's Jackson comment. Okay, me slipping with Liv; Jack's Jackson cover was actually pretty decent.

"Sorry, I meant Olivia. It's just instinctual," I say. "Maybe that's the salesman in me."

Tim smiles. "Always on, this guy, always on," he says to everyone.

Liv takes another sip of her drink; I see her gulp this time. "Don't worry, Liv is fine," she says. "And likewise, Christian. Good to see you again." Then she turns her head quickly in the other direction to continue conversation with Liana.

Tim never bothers to introduce me to Molly, so I take the opportunity to switch focus and say hi to her. She looks happy. Her and Undercuffler sit together like two birds in a nest, harmless, maybe, but keeping watch from above, certainly.

Why would Liv invite these friends? She has to know what she is doing. She knows I'm here. Is she trying to set me up? Is she trying to test me? Why do I even care? I'm here for business, not Liv, I should just be moving on.

Jack breaks my thoughts with a comment about Emma. "She looks good, dude," he whispers. "And don't worry, I didn't spill the beans."

I ignore the comment. Not because I don't want to respond, but just to keep a cool image. My curiosity is killing me, though.

I turn to Tim. "So how did these two end up here?"

"When Liv came back from shopping, I insisted her friends stay for dinner," Tim says with a raised voice. There goes the quiet. "I mean, it's not every day we have two young bachelors staying with us."

It's true. I have no choice but to laugh. The girls don't seem to mind, even though it's sort of at their expense. They seem to like the attention. It settles my nerves and answers the lingering question in my mind. Liv isn't behind them coming at all. This is Tim's doing.

The cocktail hour goes just fine, and dinner is excellent. Everyone has their best costumes on, wearing their masks, and is playing nice. It would be too dangerous any other way, so I'm thankful for that.

The alcohol does provide a lubricious component to an evening; slippery when wet seems to apply to many aspects of life. This is one of my big concerns. With each drink down, I lose more of my ability to control the situation and my actions. Drinking is a given, though, so like a skydiver I need blind faith.

Everywhere I look there is a fuckin' liability. Liv, Emma, and Jack know the truth. Undercuffler and Molly are basically the police. Tim is, well, Tim, and Liana is the only one who is completely oblivious. Between the gin and her sex appeal, she starts to feel like the escape route. A logical move in a sea of many illogical choices. A move everyone would expect me to take, especially as Jack starts to get closer with Emma, making up for the last time. It leaves everyone coupled up.

I want to steal Liv, put on some rock 'n' roll, and live a little, but that just isn't going to happen. Tim by her side is hard to watch; when he kisses her cheek I want to gag. Liana represents the perfect refuge. Well, her and more gin, so that's what I gravitate toward.

With the glaze spread over my eyes, it is rather easy to pull up next to Liana on the sofa. She is engulfed in her cellphone, but I think I can win that competition.

"So . . . you didn't talk much during dinner," I say to her.

"I'm a little shy around new people," Liana says, still looking at her phone.

"But you're *not* shy?" I see the earliest beginnings of a smile.

"No, I'm not shy."

"I can tell."

"You can tell? What's that supposed to mean? How can you tell?" she asks.

Okay, that was definitely a dumb comment. If I'm not going to lose any ground, I need to think of something fast. Think, think, think. I attempt a hail Mary and say the first thing that comes to my mind.

"Well, you radiate confidence."

She looks up from her phone. "Good save," she continues. "Nobody has ever said that to me before. Most people say, 'You're hot,' or, 'You're beautiful.' It's not that I don't get flattered, but those comments just get old."

Maybe I'm a bit cynical, but there's no way this woman doesn't like getting called beautiful. Her fake boobs, eyelashes, and nails signal she is trying way too hard to not enjoy being called beautiful. Not to mention the contouring done on her face. Plus, who doesn't enjoy a compliment? It just strikes me as if she's trying to make herself sound virtuous or something. Little does she know, I'm conditioned by the underworld, just gimme some truth.

Wait a minute—gimme some truth? Damn it! Just like that, Liv is all I can imagine. I look back into the kitchen and see her. She's looking directly at me as if she's been watching the whole time. I turn back to the conversation. Honestly, what does she expect?

I look at Liana and smile. "Well, I meant it." She smiles from ear to ear.

Apparently that's all I need to say, she gets more engaged, and we get lost in conversation for 20 minutes. It's mostly surface level nonsense, but I need something besides alcohol to distract my mind.

I do have empathy for Liana, or at least that's the narrative I'm spinning right now—anything could get old, even beauty. It also works for the moment. I mean, beauty is great in the moment. What? I'm not making sense. Shit, my head is spinning.

When I look at the clock, it's already midnight. That's normally pretty early for me, but it was a travel day, so I am getting tired. I resume chatting with Liana for about five or ten minutes, mostly about nothing, and, when I look up again, I notice Jack and Emma are missing. Molly is gone, too. Undercuffler, Tim, and Liv are all chatting in the kitchen. Is that kiss-ass making his move? Bastard.

Liv is sneaking glances toward Liana and I every chance she gets. I want her to know that it's her I wish is on this couch, but I have to give that idea up. Take what I can get. Just roll with it.

So, I walk into the kitchen and make another drink for Liana and me. It doesn't take long for Undercuffler to say something stupid, "So, how's it going over there?"

I know what he means, but give me a break. Liv grimaces and says, "Yeah, Christian. How's it going over there?"

I give it back to them. "It's only midnight and all you old people are dropping like dominos. Someone has to keep the party going."

Undercuffler says, "I'm not that much older than you, big guy."

"You might as well be," I say.

Undercuffler does one of those dumb one-huff laughs.

"Hey, hey. It was a travel day," Tim says. "We're all a bit tired. Plus, tomorrow we're going on the boat."

That takes me by surprise. "The boat? What boat?"

Tim says, "Well, I'm telling you now, buddy."

Liv gets up to talk to Liana. I have no clue what they're saying to each other, but they're pointing and shrugging. Liv looks back into the kitchen with a stare that could see through concrete. Thankfully nobody else sees it. It's pointed directly at me. Then she turns back to Liana, gives her the same look, and bolts up the stairs.

The alcohol is giving me courage. "Looks like Olivia is the next domino," I say to Tim.

"Ha—yeah, she had a long day. We're about to call it a night as well," he says, then moves a little closer and lowers his voice "Listen. I don't care what you do or how late you're up. But just remember that's my wife's friend."

Why is that everyone immediately assumes I have the worst intention? Christ, he's the one who insisted they stay in the first place. "I got it. I got it," I say. "We're good."

I walk back into the living room, hand Liana her drink, sit next to her, and notice a small frown on her face. "What's wrong?" I ask.

"I hate when people try to control me."

"What do you mean?"

"I can make my own decisions about my life," she says. "Olivia wanted to get an Uber for me, but I told her I'm going to hang for a little while because I'm enjoying your company."

Liana takes a sip of her drink then puts it back on the table in front of her. "It just felt weird. She seemed a little upset that I wanted to stay. I insisted I was okay and reminded her that I drove here. Why invite me and then tell me to leave?"

I want to tell her, technically, Liv didn't invite her, Tim did, but I'm not about to go down that road. I know what's really going on here with Liv. I take the high road and don't get tangled in their dispute.

"You know, she is probably just trying to be a good friend," I say. "I wouldn't read too much into it."

"You're probably right," she says. "Sorry to kill the convo. Where were we?"

All the signals point toward Liv still being emotionally attached. I'm relieved to know she cares, even though I know I shouldn't be.

But I'm a long way from being able to understand Liv's feelings. I'm well-oiled and alone with a woman who has rock-hard nipples blasting through her skimpy sundress. Not just any woman, either, a woman with a slight

vendetta against Liv trying to control her. The worst way
to get someone to do something is by telling them to do it.
I almost wish Liv had been a little more savvy with Liana;
Liv could have saved me from myself. Now I'm powerless
in the grasp of evil and in the name of fun.

Everyone has gone to sleep, anything I'm saying seems
to land. Liana and I are giddy like schoolchildren. In
between one of the laughs, we sneak a kiss which seems to
light up her eyes. Everything appears set. All I have to do is
ask the question, so I ask it. "You want to go to my room?"

Her response is as predictable as the sun that will rise
in five hours. She just looks at me and nods with a smile.

She asks, "Where's the bathroom?" The famous last
words of every woman ever getting ready to sleep with
someone for the first time. In the meantime, I head into my
room.

Just like the March sun that tricks beachgoers in New
England, beauty has always been my downfall. I jump the
gun and wind up in my swim trunks during 50-degree
weather. I close the blinds that cover the floor-to-ceiling
sliding doors, then sit on the edge of my bed. It gives me
too much time to consider what is about to happen.
Although completely justified in every sense, something
inside is still questioning it. The delay is making me hem
and haw about actually sleeping with Liana. I remember a
Bob Dylan line, "You can always come back, but you can't
come back all the way." It rattles me. Not knowing what to
do, I look at my phone on the nightstand and read a text
message from my Father, "Enjoy the trip. Proud of you.
Dad."

Ahh, that is the final nail in my coffin. I don't have the
balls to say I can't go through with it. I don't have a good
enough reason. Actually, I don't have any reason, except

the one that doesn't make sense to anyone but me. I don't want to hurt Liv. Shit, why am I being such a wussy?

I lay my head back and close my eyes and pretend to be asleep. I hear Liana open the door and close it. She tries to wake me with some mating calls, a push, a shake, and a whisper, but I ignore each attempt.

I hear her murmur under her breath, "You've got to be kidding me."

She makes a few last attempts to wake me by gently poking me in the side. On her second poke, I open my left eye, pretending like I'm out of it. I say with a raspy tone, "I must have fallen asleep. What time is it?"

She just looks at me with no response.

"Lay down," I mumble. "Rest a little. You've been drinking."

After a moment, she says, "Move over."

I roll over and the clock on the nightstand reads 2am. I know I need to get her on the road before the sun comes up.

THIRTEEN

IT'S A DEAD SILENT MORNING. One of those mornings where even the clouds are wondering why you're out of bed. "Look, at this idiot," they whisper to each other. I feel like screaming, "I don't want to get up," but that might wake everyone. I only have about 30 minutes before sunrise. I've got to get Liana out of here *and* I could use some coffee. Now it's my turn to poke Liana.

I nudge her. "Liana. Liana."

She awakes in a daze, squints, mumbles, and admits it is best that she gets out of here before anyone else opens their eyes. "You passed out last night," she tells me. I knew this was coming, so I'm not taken back.

"I guess I had one too many drinks," I say. "Maybe it was best."

"That's one way of looking at it," she says. "Or a missed opportunity."

I grin. "I know. I know. It wasn't exactly good timing on my part. There's always next time?"

"I guess we'll see. You can take my number."

I take it, but know I'll never call her. Last night, I

escaped that scenario by the skin of my teeth. The last thing I'm going to do is jump back into that pressure cooker and hang out with her again. I know she's local, so I ask her, "Are there any coffee shops around here?"

"There's a little one about five minutes from here."

"Can I walk there?"

"You can, but I wouldn't," she says. "I can take you."

Fuck, I don't want her to come back with me.

"You can just drop me off and I'll grab a car back. Don't want to inconvenience you."

"It's really not a big deal," she says.

I just look at her for about 20 seconds, raise my eyebrows, open my eyes wide, and she gets the point. She understands the optics, and agrees to drop me off and then head home.

As I close the passenger door to Liana's car and head into the coffee shop, I look back to see her yawn. "Thanks for a great night," I say.

"Call me sometime," she says.

I know that might be the last time I see her, so I savor the moment. I have to say, she does look beautiful, even in her tired morning state. A shame that she'll never hear me tell her. Oh well, so long pal, I say to myself. So long.

I look up and see a wooden sign that reads, "Sun's Up Coffee." It seemed fitting, seeing as the sun is literally just starting to rise. Geez, how many people have had that thought?

The cafe is tiny, a little box of a place with the delectable smell of freshly ground coffee beans. An older gentleman is behind the counter and greets me almost immediately as I walk through the door.

"Morning, amigo," he says. "What would you like?"

"Gimme just a minute." My brain still isn't firing on all cylinders and I want a little more time to scan the menu.

"Take your time," he says. "We're not going anywhere."

There are two tables on either side of the square-shaped room. A man is reading a paper at the right corner table, the only one in front of a window. The window on the left side is covered with a sign that reads, "Ice Cold Coffee." Only in Florida, only in Florida.

Coffee is meant to be hot, especially in the morning. I don't care where I am or how hot it is outside. People who drink cold coffee confuse me, maybe I can understand drinking it in the afternoon, but not in the morning. You need the heat in the morning just as much as you need the caffeine. And, if you have the option, always a mug over a to-go cup. It's sturdier and makes you feel like you're doing something important. After all, that's why you're drinking the coffee in the first place. To wake up. Nothing wakes you up like hot coffee in a mug. It's important.

"Hey man, do I know you?" the guy in the corner says. His voice has a deep, gravelly, gruff tone. I look over my right shoulder and he's peering above the edge of a print edition of *The New York Times*.

"I don't know, do you?" I reply.

He lowers the paper all the way down, places it on the table, and eyes me over the top of his reading glasses.

Holy shit. It's the same guy who was at the Fatty Duck with Emma, the same guy Liv hoped I'd meet. I can't remember his name, though. John Varvatos? No, that's not it. He still looks like that, too. Beaded bracelets, long hair, scruffy beard, two necklaces, short-sleeve button-down with three or four buttons undone, but he's been Florida-ized, wearing Bermuda shorts and flip-flops.

I can tell he still can't place me. Since he saw me with Liv, I have two options: one, pretend I never met him and choose to not add any more chaos to my life, or two, introduce myself. I remember Liv saying I'm like him, or something like that. It's like she hoped I met him. Right before I respond, I see he's drinking coffee from a mug. That sells me. So, I go with option two.

"We never met before," I say. "You were at the Fatty Duck up in Connecticut a couple weeks back."

He scratches his head. "The Fatty Duck?"

"You're friends with Emma and Liv, right? You were talking with Emma in the bar."

"Holy smokes," he says. "Right, and you were talking with Liv."

"Yeah."

"Grab a seat, man. What's your name?"

"Christian. You?"

"People call me Ty." He continues, "So what brings you to Florida, man?"

I don't really know how to respond. It isn't exactly the easiest thing to explain. Nor do I know how much I am willing to reveal. I shrug, then say, "It's a bit complicated."

"Isn't it always, man?" he says.

"Well, the situation I'm currently in is anything but simple. That's for sure." Ty takes a sip of coffee and he recollects something.

"Wait—don't tell me. You're not here with . . . really, man?" he asks. Liv told me that Ty could be trusted, but I am still a little uneasy. I cut him off.

"Whatever you're thinking, yes and no," I say. "Technically, I'm here with Tim, but, yes, Liv is here too."

"I'm going to get another coffee for this one, man." Ty raises his hand and yells, "Luis, refill, por favor!"

He comes over promptly, fills Ty's mug to the brim, and tops mine off too.

I decide to tell Ty the story, well, for the most part. I tell him that night was the first night I met her, we hit it off, had no idea it was Tim's wife, my boss, I ended up winning the trip, and that's why I'm here. I leave out the part about me having sex with Liv twice.

"Do you like her, man?"

"She's my boss's wife."

He raised his finger. "Tisk. Tisk. That's not what I asked. You like her. It's okay, man." He takes a sip of coffee. "Damn! That's hot." He touches his lip. He puts the mug down and continues, "Remember this: In this life we always want what we can't have."

There's something about Ty that really holds my attention. I can't quite figure this guy out and I sell shit for a living. People are kind of my thing. Is it the fact that he says "man" after nearly every sentence? Nah, that is actually a little weird. He is a little bit mysterious and a little bit witty. Maybe that is all part of it, too. I can't really put my finger on it. In any case, maybe he's right: maybe I just want Liv because I can't have her.

I use the brief pause in our chat to change topics. I tap the paper that is sitting on the table between us.

"*The New York Times*, huh?"

He smirks. "It's the best few bucks I spend all week, man."

"I didn't even realize you can get the paper shipped to you daily."

"Of course you can, what planet you livin' on." He grins and continues, "You know, it's the only thing I read these days. I can't watch that bullshit on TV. I watch a movie here and there, but the internet just moves too fast for me, man."

I look out the window, see the palm trees waving, and cars zipping by. The aroma of the coffee roasting helps to liven my senses, not just my smell, but that aroma just does something to me.

"What do you read, man?" Ty asks.

"That's a good question," I say. "I don't read much."

"So, what do you do, man?" he asks.

"What do you mean, 'what do I do?'"

"Well, if you don't read, what do you do with your time?"

"I guess I read sometimes and listen to news sound bites on my commute to work each morning. I'm a big Yankees fan, always have been since I was kid, so I follow them. I listen to music, chase women, and I work." I pause to think for a second, take a sip of coffee; Ty's right, it is hot.

Then I continue, "I still hang with friends, but not as much. My time is limited. I try to see my folks on the weekends. Oh, and I play the guitar. That's pretty much it. Is that good enough?"

"I don't know, man," he says. "You tell me, is it?"

This guy's confusing me a little. He stares at me for a second longer and then says, "Maybe you should read *The New York Times*, man."

"I guess I could," I say. "I do see people reading it every day on the train."

"It's easy. All you have to do is pick it up. You'll read about your boys in pinstripes, and also a lot of other things."

"Why do you read *The Times*, though?"

"You want me to tell you why I read *The Times*, man?" I'm actually on the edge of my chair.

"Of course," I say.

Ty takes a couple sips of coffee, looks out the window, then back at me. "It finally cooled down, man," he says.

I motion to him to answer my question. "So . . . ?"

"Right, so I was saying . . . " he says, then pauses. "*The*

Times is part of my consumption diet, man." I squish my forehead and squint my eyes.

"Consumption diet?"

"Yeah, man. A consumption diet," he says.

"You'll have to explain this one to me," I say.

"Most people don't realize they spend their entire day, actually, entire life consuming stuff," he says. "It's easy to do in America. People think too much weight kills so they go on a food diet. Well, I think too much consumption kills. You can't see it happening, but, over time, your brain gets rotten like an apple left out in this Florida sun. I've seen good people over the years kill themselves with too much consumption, man."

I've never heard anything quite like this before. The cars driving by keep distracting me and grabbing my attention. I look back at Ty. We sit silent for a moment.

"You got nothing to say, huh, man?" he says.

"I'm still not too sure what a consumption diet is, Ty."

Ty takes off his glasses and rests them on the table. "Just look at what you told me, man. You consume the Yankees, music, women, and even work. You play the guitar too."

"I do."

"Do you ever play for people?" he asks.

"Sometimes, but not much."

"You even consume the guitar, man!" he says, his voice getting louder. He shakes his head.

"I'm not saying don't do those things, you gotta live life, Lord knows I have, but how many of those things exist without you, man?" he asks.

I'm perplexed and stifled on what to say next, so I just sit with my mouth shut.

"Yankees exist without you. The music exists without you. The women you chase exist without you. The guitar exists without you. Even your job, man, it exists without you," he says.

The rabbit hole he seems to be going down is leaving me even more confused and concerned. "Doesn't everything exist without me though?" I ask.

Ty runs his hand through his long hair, then raises his finger. "Not everything, man." He takes a sip of coffee. "You told me you don't see your friends as much anymore and your folks only on some weekends. Partner? Kids? Siblings?"

"Just one brother."

"How often do you see him?" he asks.

Honestly, at this moment I can't remember the last time we saw each other. I'm reluctant to say, "Almost never."

"All those relationships you're neglecting are creations that can't exist without you," he says. "That guitar you play, maybe you just want to play for a hobby, that's cool. Enjoy it, please do, but play it for people. Create something that can't exist without you, man."

I finally find the courage to open my mouth. "Why are you telling me all this?" I ask.

He chuckles. "Do you know what I do?"

"No."

"I'm a 59-year-old guitar player, man."

"Really?"

"Yeah, man," he says. "I've been a session guitarist most of my life. I've played all over the world. I've played with everyone from Michael Jackson to Sir Paul McCartney."

Holy shit. Did he just say Paul . . . he definitely did. Who is this guy? I've heard about session musicians before, but I don't really know much about them, so I ask him, "What's a session guitarist?"

"Well, I play in the studio when people are recording and sometimes onstage when artists need guitarists. Good ones," he says and smiles. "I've spent my whole life playing the guitar. I won't lie to you, I love it, and it's been great to me. How do you think I bought this house in Golden Beach?" He goes on, "I've made a lot of money playing other people's music, man. But let me tell you something," he says leaning in.

"Of course."

"The most alive I ever felt was when I was creating my own music with my own band, even if the world doesn't know who the fuck I am, man."

Damn—now here's an honesty you don't get every day. It's not hard to imagine Ty's danced with the underworld. I laugh to myself.

"I bet you traveled a lot though, huh? I imagine you severed some relationships along the way?" I ask.

"Too many," he says. "Chased a lot of women around, still do. Cocaine, booze, party, fun, all that stuff, man," he snickers as he says this. "I only ended up down here because of Clapton's *461 Ocean Boulevard* album. That's Golden Beach. After he got hooked on the junk, he escaped down here, I never got lost on H, but I thought if Golden Beach was good enough for Clapton, fuck it, it will be good enough for me. Only few people have ever played the guitar like Clapton. You know what I mean, man?"

"I do know what you mean. He's a technical beast on the guitar and I love that blues sound."

He chuckles and repeats, "A technical beast on the guitar, man."

I wish I could talk to this guy all day. I feel like there is still so much to talk about with him. I haven't even asked him anything about guitar and I want some stories, but I know I have to get back to the house. I'm reminded when I look at my cellphone and see a text message from Jack that reads, "Where the fuck are ya?"

Time has been passing, my coffee is starting to near empty, and the real world is calling my name. I have to depart this shamanic mountain and re-enter civilization. Fuck me. I order an Uber and look back at Ty.

"I don't even know what to say," I tell Ty.

He looks over at me, smiles bright, and itches his beard. "Don't say nothing," he says. "Let's just go back to your original question, man." I nod my head, pretending to remember what it was, but I can't. He continues, "You know, about reading *The New York Times*, man?"

"Yeah, the consumption diet?" I say.

"Yes, you got it, man."

I see my Uber pull up, so I know I have to go. "Great talking with you. See you around."

"Well, you know where to find me," he says. "I'm here every morning that I'm in town. Even if I've had a long night." I just smirk. I can tell he's had many nights go past 4am.

I stand up and push my chair in. Ty puts *The Times* back up in front of his face, and goes right back to what he was doing before I stumbled through the door. Just as I'm about to walk out, I hear his rough voice.

"Christian."

I turn back to look at him.

"One last thing, man."

"Yeah, what's that, Ty?"

"Always remember to look at what's directly in front of you," he says. "God speed, man, God speed."

As I get in the back seat of the Uber, a small sedan, Ty's last comment sinks to the bottom of my gut like an anchor holding me in thought for the entire drive back. I have to roll the window down just so the breeze can cool off my overheating brain.

I think about my immediate future—the promotion. I have Tim's voice playing in my mind, "You can have all this." Undoubtedly, it is a life of comfort. But, do I even want "all this?"

A beautiful house bought in desperation to save a marriage. The cheating wife. The suit and tie every day for the rest of my life. I feel like an asshole, because I'm grateful for the opportunity Tim is offering me. The money, security, would be nice, and being Undercuffler's boss is a double bonus. It might be possible to have all that without Tim's shitty situation, but maybe Ty is onto something. Maybe I can't escape the inevitabilities that come along with the path. I mean, that's what he meant, right?

My Dad pops into my mind, how proud he'll be, even if he doesn't say it, when I tell him, "Hey Dad, I got a promotion." It's the recognition I want and feel I deserve. Now I have the recognition, but Ty's voice continues to bang off the walls of my mind like a ping-pong ball, back 'n' forth, volley for volley.

The breeze coming through the cracked back window goes from refreshing to tepid and the car slows to a stop outside the house.

The day is already one I would not soon forget, but the sight of Tim and Liv in the driveway packing some things into their Jeep is a reminder it is only beginning. It's a cold shot of reality with enough oomph to pry that anchor loose. Fuck, off I go.

Tim turns, sees me getting out of the car, and yells out, "Christian, where have you been? Come grab some breakfast before we head on the boat for the day!"

And Liv, she doesn't even turn around.

FOURTEEN

I sit on the bow of the boat with both arms draped around my bent knees and look out onto the water, the infinite sea of the unknown. The water is calm, neither a wave nor a jumping fish wanting to disturb the peace on the ocean surface. What lies underneath is anyone's guess.

The boat glides along with the tide, the only rumbling is inside me, the eggs and bacon from breakfast are swirling around in my stomach. Even in calm waters, there's nothing worse than being on a boat with an upset stomach. But the beautiful panorama before me keeps the grumbling at bay. There's a clear view of the horizon off in the distance and the waterscape is mesmerizing sprawled out in front of me. It's still and quiet for the moment. Ah, peaceful.

Tim chartered an 80-foot yacht from 10am to 4pm. It is pretty sweet. The yacht has three levels, six beds, a kitchen, fully stocked bar, TVs everywhere, a living area, and even one jet ski in the back.

Most importantly, at least right now, it has four bathrooms. This is plenty to find a quiet one, always important in a public place. I hate being rushed and anxious on the toilet. Honestly, who likes that?

The boat is fully furnished and minted with brand new accessories. It can't be more than a year or two old. I'd say it probably cost about $5,000-$6,000 for the six- hour charter, not including the private chef. Is it excessive? Yes. But considering that Tim probably pays the same amount in taxes per month on that Golden Beach home, it doesn't seem terribly excessive. It actually seems right in line with everything else, you know, showing Undercuffler and I how much he appreciates us. What life could be like for us. Maybe he is being genuine, but I have Ty in the back of my mind. There's a lot of consumption going on around me, but damn, I'm enjoying it.

I hear a shout from somewhere above, "This is fuckin' gorgeous, ain't it!?" I look up and Jack is leaning on the rail on another deck and—no surprise—I can see a drink in his hand. It's only 10.30am, but now I wonder if everyone is drinking already. He shouts again, "Come up here!"

I sure can use a mimosa, but first I have to take care of some business. "I'll be up in a minute. Got hit the head!" I yell back.

I begin my descent below the deck, can't wait to drop this bathing suit down to my ankles, but I hit some turbu- lence along the way. My knees shake, I can recognize those shoulders anywhere, Liv is tying on her sequin cover-up. It's not covering much, both her white bikini and sun- kissed skin are screaming through, she's looking godly.

Just the idea we're both in the same room with that much skin showing makes my little friend down below start to move. She looks at me for the first time all day.

"Did you have a good time last night?" she says.

It doesn't take a genius to understand where she is going with this line of questioning, so I jump the gun.

"Look, it's not what you think. I . . . "

Liv cuts me off. "What is it? You come to my house, sleep with my friend, and enjoy my husband's praise. I get it, Christian. I do," she says. "Like the situation you're in, but you don't have to rub it in my face."

"Sleep with your friend?"

"C'mon don't bullshit me," Liv says. "I heard Mark joking with the guys this morning. He was up at 4am to get some water and Liana's car was still in the driveway."

I want to rebut this point, but I feel a drag race about to go off in my stomach. Start your engines. Three . . . two . . . I muster up, "Look, it's not what you think. I swear, but I'll be right back."

Liv shakes her head and sighs. "Be right back?"

"I gotta use the bathroom!"

"Of course you do," I hear her say under her breath.

I go down one more level into the sleeping quarters to find a nice quiet bathroom. Ah, found one, perfect to collect myself. Fuckin' Undercuffler. That spiny little shit. Time to prepare for an uphill battle.

I come back upstairs and, no surprise, Liv is back out on the main deck. At least, I'm feeling better now. The first person I see when I get up there is Undercuffler. He says, "It's great down here in Florida, isn't it?"

He doesn't know he just screwed me, so I can't really hold a grudge, but he's still a prick. "No doubt," I say with a smile.

Tim is up on the flybridge talking to the captain with a Bloody Mary in his hand. Emma, Liv, and Molly are sitting together, sipping mimosas outside on the back of the boat. Undercuffler excuses himself to try to get some cell service to make a call. It gives me time to go catch up with Jack, he's standing alone under the overhang in the bar area.

"You're never going to believe this shit," I say.

"Oh God. What now?" he says.

"Liv thinks I slept with Liana last night."

"You didn't?"

"No, dude!"

"Mark was telling Tim and me this morning . . . "

I cut him off. "I know what Undercuffler was telling you, but he's a dumb-ass. That doesn't mean I had sex with her."

He looks up in the air, raises his hand toward the sky, then looks back at me. "Wait—so you didn't poke her?"

"No! That's what I'm telling you!"

"What's wrong with you!?" Jack says. "Ah, suit yourself. I'll tell you what, though. That chick Emma is a handful. If you know what I mean."

"Nothing is wrong with me. And I thought she was too old for you?"

He laughs. "Me too. Who knew?"

Tim yells down from above, "Who wants to take the jet ski for a spin?"

I look at Jack, Jack looks at me, and we both point at each other. "There ya go, buddy," I say. "Take your love-bird out for a spin."

He takes a sip of his cocktail. "Good idea," then howls out, "Emma, you want to go for a spin on the jet ski?"

She howls back, "What!?"

I push Jack and say, "Just go over there."

He walks over, before you know it, they hop on the wave runner and zip off.

We are down by the port of Miami. It's full of cruise ships and cargo boats, and the city skyline sits in the background. Huge residential homes with Spanish tile roofs, in-ground pools line the small islands around us, each home equipped with their own yacht resting at their dock. A few party boats float in the water, stacked to the gills with 20-

somethings. Music blaring, hair swinging, and beer splashing higher than the water.

It's noon, and sun is blazing directly above us. Tim comes tumbling down the spiral stairs from the flybridge and grabs me by the shoulders.

"This is the life, huh?" he says with a grin that would impress a clown. I shake my head and smile. He continues, "Just a beautiful day with my top guys! What can be better?" We clink glasses.

Jack and Emma are getting back from their spin on the water.

"You gotta get out there, Christian! It's great," Jack yells.

Tim leans over to me. "I don't go on those things. I had a bad experience when I was younger."

"What's that?" I ask.

"Someone freaking hit me while I was riding one. I was fortunate nothing bad happened, but I guess it kind of traumatized me for life."

"Holy shit," I say. "That's terrible."

I can't help but wonder if his hesitancy might also have something to do with losing his daughter in a motor vehicle accident.

Undercuffler is a chicken shit. He doesn't want to go on the jet ski either. I don't expect anything else from a stiff. Whatever, more time for Jack or me to enjoy it. I'm eager to jump on.

As I strap on the life vest, I hear Tim screech out, "Olivia, you always want me to take you. Why don't you go for a ride with Christian?"

I think she almost spits out her drink mid-sip. She pauses. "I think I'm good."

Jack being an asshole yells out, "Are you sure? It's gorgeous out there."

Emma chimes in, "Yeah, Olivia. You have to go! You always want to go."

What the hell? But before I know it, everyone on the boat is chanting, "Olivia, Olivia, Olivia, Olivia." I watch the madness as I sit on the jet ski with my life vest on. It only takes about 30 seconds of child-like chanting to get Liv to slam her drink down. "Fine! I'll go!"

It's true she was holding her ground for a little while, but there's no way she would agree if she didn't want to go out on the water with me. I take comfort in the thought, even if I shouldn't, or am wrong. I've done all I can to avoid Liv up until this point, and now her bare skin is going to be pressed up against mine. The transfer of heat might be dangerous. It's like rubbing together two sticks and hoping for science to fail you. It doesn't seem plausible.

She hops on the back and whispers, "Make this a short ride."

I look over my shoulder. "I never thought I'd hear you say that one." I have to take the shot.

She pokes my side. "Stop. Let's go!"

I look up to the boat, nobody is even paying attention, including Tim. Nobody seems to care about Liv and me. But why would they, I guess? It feels like we've been abandoned, left alone, and that thought is enough for me to twist the throttle and blast off out onto the water.

Liv grips me tight and screams in my right ear, giving me flashbacks that only make me hammer on that throttle more aggressively. For a moment, I imagine I'm on a motorcycle, a Harley or something, and Liv and I are ripping down the interstate. I'm not sure there's a more liberating thought than the open road with a lady friend by your side. The possibilities feel endless and opportunities seem fruitful, even if you're doomed, it's the hope that keeps you moving forward.

The water splashing pulls me back to the present. We've only been on the jet ski for a few minutes and our boat is already far in the distance.

Perhaps this is going to be the only chance I get to set the record straight about Liana, I think. Although it probably doesn't matter, I want Liv to know the truth. That's why I didn't go through with it. Even though we are far enough away from the boat that no one can really see us, I still pull the jet ski around a little rock face to block any visibility. The highest precautions must be taken so not even binoculars can spot us. Sure, it isn't an ideal situation, but I have to make the most of it. She doesn't seem surprised when I stop the jet ski and hover in the water.

I look back over my shoulder. Liv's hair is wet, eyes covered with her big, round sunglasses, and beads of water running down the lenses. I twist my upper body and adjust myself on the seat so I'm more sideways. My right shoulder nestles up against Liv's life vest.

"Look, I need to tell you something," I say. "I know it doesn't matter, but it matters to me that you know I didn't sleep with Liana. You can think whatever you want, but the truth is I was going to sleep with her, but I couldn't bring myself to do it. I actually pretended like I passed out just to avoid it. She slept at the house because she'd been drinking."

My heart is racing, so I pause for a second. "It's true, I tried to get her out of the house early, but only to avoid . . . this conversation and misunderstanding. Obviously, that didn't happen. You can even ask her when you see her."

Liv lowers her sunglasses, the sun makes her eyes glisten, those little emeralds burn straight to my soul. "Why,

Christian?" she asks. "Why didn't you just sleep with her? It would have made this so much easier."

I'm confused for a minute, but what she says has an element of truth. "Well, why didn't you just pretend to not care I was with Liana? That would have made it easier on me!"

Liv stalls. She grabs her drenched hair, rings it out, then lets off a big sigh. She removes her sunglasses and doesn't say a word. I look into her eyes, but only briefly, they now have a pink hue. We sit silent for about a minute, me looking forward and Liv's chin on my right shoulder. It's sad, but perfect. It's in this moment I realize the only thing shining brighter than the sun today is the truth about our feelings for each other. I didn't just sleep with my boss's wife. It's much worse. I might be in love with her. Fuck!

"What am I going to do with you, Christian?" she says after a moment longer.

"What am I going to do with you, Liv?" I reply.

I can feel her heart on my shoulder through the life jacket, beating faster, and faster. Science did not fail us, and the early beginning of a fire is rising.

I feel her right hand start to slide down between my legs. A shock wave travels through my body with such force it makes my toes curl.

She whispers in my right ear, "Shh. Don't talk. I want to feel you one more time."

She slips her tongue in my ear and grasps my penis fiercely with her right hand. It's dancing. The combination makes the hair on the back of my neck stand up. Then her strong grip loosens and soft lips kiss the lobe of my ear. It's both a dream and a nightmare. Then, just as quickly, she whispers, "Let's get back."

I look back at her. "Really?"

She just beams at me, then covers those sinners with

her shades. I'm disappointed, but I have no choice, we can't be gone too long.

We haven't been on the ride too long, maybe 15 minutes, but I don't want to raise any suspicion either. Plus, I don't know what to make of all this. Maybe escaping the moment is the best decision. I hit the throttle, zoom off, and Liv's body sticks to mine, now superglued together as we rip through the open water. The only thing I hear, though, is the sound of Liv's beating heart against my back. I try to bask in the fleeting moment, but her heart is playing the sweetest song for me and the ride goes by even quicker.

The music begins to skip like a scratched record and the bravado of a man's voice breaks the soft notes that guided me back to the boat.

"You're back already!?" Tim shouts from the boat as we arrive.

Maybe we haven't been gone as long as I thought. A side-effect of guilt, possibly. I wish I had taken more time. Damn it.

Molly and Emma simultaneously blurt out, "Did you have fun?"

"It was fun," Liv says. "Different from what I expected."

Tim laughs. "Was she a lot to handle?" he asks.

That comment makes the guilt swirl inside me. How can I answer that question? I put myself in this situation, though. Was it worth it? I suppose. At least I'm not the initiator. Not this time, anyway. It's the only way I'll be able to make peace with it.

"She was fine, Tim," I say.

Jack and Emma's eyes are telling a different story than anyone else's.

Some time passes, and we are all sitting down to eat a late lunch. I'm not in the mood to drink after the morning cocktails, so I nurse one Tom Collins for most of the day and enjoy the surface-level chatting with everyone. I only want to punch Undercuffler in the face once. I consider that an achievement. Most of my thinking is about what happened on the jet ski. Liv is very ginger around me. I expect nothing less, though. I really want to tell her I met Ty, but I don't know how to bring it up. What would Ty say? I can't decide whether he'd tell me to go all in or pull back.

I zone out watching the cook flip hamburgers and, just like ground beef, every element of my predicament seems to be intrinsically linked with bacteria, quite honestly, that's the hardest part. There are potential issues everywhere. In that way, maybe my burger isn't even getting cooked; I'm willingly eating a raw one.

FIFTEEN

AFTER A LONG DAY on the water, everyone rests up at the house so they can make the most of the evening. Tim wants to take Undercuffler and I out for a "guys" night in Miami. Under most circumstances, this would be right up my alley. A perfect city to dance with the Devil, Luke Handleys everywhere, and debauchery waiting on every corner. In Miami, there's a natural sex appeal that drips into the water supply. It taps the city's main vein and leaks out of every pore. You can't escape it.

I just want to make it to the morning, creep out of bed at 6am, and go one more round with Ty. At this rate, I'll be lucky to be home by 6am. That's Miami at its best, though. People say they love coffee, too, then, when you dig a bit deeper, you find out they're drinking it with milk and sugar. If that's coffee, then Miami might just be Boca Raton. Or worse, you find out they're drinking decaf; might as well be Naples at that point. You can always run into some stiff who wants to be all politically correct, "Well there's a lot of ways you can experience Miami." This is true, but there's only one way it's meant to be experienced. That's why it exists the way it does. And once you've had it that way, anything else just feels like fake coffee.

This is my problem, I know Miami and every ounce of pleasure that goes with it. An unrelenting stimulation factory that tempts you even while you're eating the main course. So, like I say, under normal circumstances this kind of decadence would be perfect for a "guys" night. But don't be fooled, this meant a "girls" night had the potential to be just as scandalous. Miami has an equal effect on both men and women. Actually, that's what makes it so dangerous. With all that being, Liv, Molly, and Emma decide to hit the town on their own as well. Of course, Jack will tag along with us.

We head to dinner at a hotspot on the Miami River called Rhythm. The name is apt because it's a restaurant that turns into a dance party. These places aren't really restaurants in the traditional sense, they're more like restaurants slash lounges, perfect for people trying to disguise their fun. Like the 1950s lounges where people sat at tables, ate dinner, and watched some performance. The tables don't actually get removed or anything. That's still your home base for the night, but as the music starts to get louder and more festive, the place no longer feels like a joint where you just ate $60 steak with a $300 bottle of wine. And once the alcohol really starts flowing, your body catches fire and you always end up wishing you were in the outfit you were born in, not some dinner attire.

Rhythm is an open-air spot. Mostly indoor, but the entire backside is exposed to the Miami River. The only thing left to cool you down is the light breeze coming off the water. It has a DJ and she has a real sense of the crowd. Her song choices tickle your toes, make you want to move, and gradually go from softer to more upbeat as the night rolls on.

It's about 11pm, and a special burlesque show ensues. The performers waft and float through the crowded tables in their provocative attire, while the music gets more dramatic and dark. It's Rhythm's way of letting you know the Devil has arrived. So instead of dinner being delivered to the table, now is the time to start having bottles of your favorite Champagne brought to you instead.

On that note, I raise my hand to signal the waitress. I look at Tim and he says, "Whatever you want, big guy." Undercuffler's eyes are glued on the show, lost-puppy syndrome, someone has to remind him they don't take singles. Jack's already walking on water. Right now, the only thing that can slow him down is another plane episode. Fuck, I don't even want to think about that.

I tell the waitress, "A couple bottles of Champagne, and a bottle of gin."

She shouts back over the music. "What kind?"

Tim hears the exchange and shouts, "The best!"

The waitress shouts, "Are you sure!?"

"Don't kill me. Just bring the good stuff. We're celebrating," he says. "Ask this guy about the gin."

"Gotcha!" she says to Tim, then looks at me. "So??"

"Monkey 47, if you got it," I say. She nods.

I realize we are already pretty tipsy from dinner and once we start to put a dent in those bottles, who knows where we might end up? I ask Undercuffler, "You having a good time?"

"I can't believe the body of this woman," he says with his eyes glued to the performer. She is stacked. Plus, she can contort her body in ways that defy gravity, and any sane man would be thinking the same thing—what she is like in the sack. Undercuffler, no doubt, is a sane man.

Jack says, "I know a place where we could see a lot of that!"

Undercuffler almost jumps, "Where!?"

I thought Undercuffler was sane, but never witty. Only a straight wouldn't know what Jack meant almost immediately.

Tim screeches out, "Me too!" Well, I guess Tim isn't a straight. Jack and Tim clearly have a titty bar on their mind.

I'd expect that from Jack, but from Tim it is a little bit of a shock. I mean, he's married to Liv. I guess it's not that big of a deal. You can see worse on television these days.

Who am I to judge? I know nothing about married life aside from what friends have told me and, of course, Jack's willful experience. We all know how that worked out. The way Liv has mentioned her current state, it's hard to imagine that she would even care. It's guy code to turn a blind eye to this stuff, anyway. A tough pill to swallow given the circumstances, I'm sort of brooding watching Tim flirt with random women. I mean, we are all flirting with women as the night progresses, and, as liquid courage starts to take hold, you become more flappable. Or how should I say it? You get loose lips.

I take the opportunity to clarify Undercuffler's snake move earlier in the day.

"*For the record*, I didn't bang Liana last night," I say over the music. "I passed out like a Dad on Thanksgiving!" Everyone cracks up.

Jack slurs, "*For the record*, I did bang Emma last night. We did awful . . . "

I cut him off. "Okay, we get the point!" Everyone laughs again.

Undercuffler yells out, "Well, I guess, *for the record*, I had sex with my wife last night!"

We raise our glasses, continue to crack up and yell, "Congrats, Mark!"

This is as pure a guy moment as they get, but here I am like a ninja in the night waiting to hear what Tim is going to say. Then, like a judge dropping his gavel, he declares, "*For the record*, I also had sex with my wife last night . . . " The weight of a hundred bricks has been dropped on my heart. He continues, " . . . and it was the first time in over a year!"

We all just sit there until Jack shouts, "Well, that explains why I hear you've been a real asshole in the office." Tim and Undercuffler both look at me. I look at Jack. Jack continues, "Just kidding!" We all erupt again in laughter, except this time my smile is plastic. Liv slept with Tim? It's her husband, but it's hard to cancel out my feelings for her. What we don't see, we don't know, so it doesn't have to be real. I heard it, though, and it became real—too real.

But there is that little wrinkle: over a year? What was that about? Could her thinking I slept with Liana have something to do with Tim finally getting laid? For the first time in over a year?

I actually feel vindication that she might have had revenge sex with her husband. A shitty feeling, but a true one nonetheless. Maybe Liv really does care about me.

Oddly, it's the only jolt I need to keep the night PG. I'm on my best behavior now. Some time passes and Jack keeps pointing at his watch then pointing to door. I say, "What?"

Jack slurs, "Strip club? We're losing time."

I shake my head and point at Tim and Undercuffler. They're both seated in their chairs, slouched over, and eyes half-closed. An old guy and a young-old guy showing their lack of stamina. Jack is trying like hell to get me to go to the titty bar, but no way I'm giving in. I just don't know what Tim might say to Liv, pillow talk, the reason for Tim being at the titty bar or something. It's common for married guys to blame their single friends for bad behavior. I don't want to be the scapegoat or the renegade outlaw. Not in this situation, I have too much at stake. I can't risk stoking Liv or Tim's fire.

We all stumble into the Golden Beach house around 3am. It's early for a Miami night, but everyone is barely standing. Hooting, hollering, and huddling around the kitchen island eating leftovers from the first couple days. I got to log in a couple hours of sleep so I can get to that coffee shop in the morning. I have to try and catch Ty one more time.

I'm about to leave the kitchen and head into the bedroom when Tim says, "One of . . . Hm . . . Well . . . " He stops, then starts again. "I completely forgot," he says. "I might have to head back tomorrow."

"Where, Rhythm?" Undercuffler says. "Me too!"

"Ha—No. New York," Tim says. I stop chewing on the cheese I'm eating, and Undercuffler looks confused while bracing himself on the kitchen island with one hand.

"New York . . . What?" I ask.

"Earlier today, I got an email from Lorelei, you know my secretary?"

We all nod.

"Well, Perkins' secretary emailed her today and told her there was a meeting EP *needs* me to be at on Monday morning." When our CEO and founder, says "jump," you ask how high, not lie down instead. If he is being summoned, Tim has no choice.

Jack says, "See we should have just stayed out tonight and made the most of it!"

"There's the door," Tim says. Jack begins to walk toward it and I rattle him in.

"He was kidding, Jack," I say.

Jack looks at me with googly eyes. "I knew that."

"Why didn't you tell us earlier?" Undercuffler asks.

"We were having such a good time I didn't want to ruin it with water cooler talk," Tim replies.

"Well, that sucks," I say.

"I guess, but I'll figure it out in the morning," Tim says. "I need some sleep." He looks at each of us. "Actually, you all do!" he shouts. "Especially this guy." He points to Jack who is eating dip with his bare fingers. I want to razz him, but my brain feels like that dip looks. Mushy.

Tim is right. It's time to rest.

SIXTEEN

THE SUN CREEPING OVER the horizon wakes me up Sunday morning. My lips are stuck together, and my mouth is stone dry; the lingering effects of one too many cocktails. Damn Tom Collins. I reach for my phone on the nightstand and check the time with one eye. Shit, it's already half past six. I gotta get to that coffee shop. I find the nearest pair of shorts, throw on the same T-shirt I wore yesterday, and a pair of sandy flip-flops.

No one's in the kitchen, so quiet you can hear a mouse run, and makes me consider how noisy I am. Six hours of sleep in two days filled with food, booze, sun, and life problems just ain't enough to keep you thinking clearly. I drink an entire liter of water waiting for the Uber.

I know the only thing that really quells the booze blues is sleep, but if I want to see Ty, time isn't exactly something I have in excess.

The Uber comes plowing into the driveway like a monster truck. It's an older pick-up with an extended cab. The driver looks like he's slept less hours than me, maybe out chasing gators all night or something.

I tell him, "Sun's Up Coffee Shop."

"I *see* it on the phone," he says. Great, he's an asshole, too. Best way to stymie an asshole is with kindness, but I have no patience for that so I just stoop to his level.

"Last night was a rough one for me," I say. "I think I woke up drunk."

He picks up a cup and hocks a loogie into it that sounds like it has been building for a week. "I hear that."

There's a stench permeating throughout the truck that I just can't ignore. Worse than a skunk—at least that smell is familiar. This is more body odor and roadkill blended together. I'm in the back cab and the pick-up is too dated, I don't have my own window. I'm trapped in a hotbox, or worse, some kind of torture chamber. The more I analyze my surroundings, the more I feel like I'm in the beginning of a horror movie. I can't even tell it's South Florida anymore. Terrible situation for a normal morning, never mind a hangover.

"Hey, do you mind cracking the window?" I ask. He doesn't say anything, just rolls the window down a little bit. Not even his open window can get rid of that horrendous smell. The slight breeze doesn't cool me down, it just moves the stink closer to my nostrils; at one point my eyes start to water.

He leans over and spits into the cup again. Why can't he just spit out the window? Only a savage dumps his phlegm in a cup next to him, when he has a window to his left. I know the coffee shop is near, so I decide to keep my mouth shut. I only see the downside—death by axe to chest or death by ingesting toxic waste. Keeping my mouth closed is the best option. Finally, one sweet word comes to my rescue. "Here," he says.

I hop out the truck with such exuberance I almost trip over my flip-flops. The smell of coffee roasting is the exact opposite of what I have just endured. It's like nose sex. I stumble to the entrance and almost rip the old wooden door straight off the hinges.

Once inside, I look over to where I expect Ty to be, but his table is empty. There's not even a used *New York Times* or anything. Actually, there's nobody in here at all. I haven't felt this let down since I found out Liv was married to Tim. There is still so much I want to ask Ty. Where is he? I didn't even get to talk to him about music or the guitar. No sleep for this? I'm tired, potentially still drunk, and all I want is to get back to bed. I look out the window and the Uber driver still hasn't left yet. I'm not getting back in that truck with that hillbilly. No way.

I hear the bathroom door slam shut. My eyes shoot up. I have the hope of a child on Christmas morning. Ty? The balloon of hope is popped. Poof. It's gone.

It's a short man, the same man who was here yesterday morning. I can't remember his name for the life of me. So, I ask him, "Hey Sir, do you remember me from yesterday?"

He puts his apron on and ties the drawstrings. "I get a lot of people, amigo," he says. "I wish I could remember everyone."

He begins to pour some beans into a large coffee grinder.

"Do you know the man who usually sits in the corner over there?" I point to Ty's table.

He snaps back, "What's it to you? You ask too many questions."

"So, you know him?"

He stops pouring the beans and points at the door.

"Do you want a coffee or not?" he shouts. "Otherwise get out of here, *pendejo*."

Why is this guy being so damn hostile with me?

"Look, Sir. I don't mean any problems. I just met him yesterday . . . here . . . "

He cuts me off. "A lot of people meet him here," he says. "He's a regular and I look out for regulars. They're family."

Truth be told, I respect that. I just really want to know where the hell Ty is and when he will be back. I can't come right out and say it, though. I might get a fist full of coffee beans on my face.

"Okay, but I sat down with him for a while, right over there yesterday. His name is Ty," I say. "And you came over and refilled our mugs. Right around the same time as now. Ty told me I can always find him here."

The man stops pouring the beans and stares at me. I'm waiting for the beans to start flying any second.

"Wait a minute—what's your name!?"

"My name is Christian."

He steps down from pouring the beans, and smiles. "Well, why the heck didn't you just say so, amigo!?"

Go figure. It almost seems too simple.

"Ty had to hit the road for a while, but he actually stopped by last night before we closed up to drop something off for you."

"He did?"

"He told me if a young guy named Christian comes back, he had something for him," he says. "Sorry, I gave you shit, amigo. Ty is who he is, you know? Sometimes we get fans or groupies in here."

Is who he is? It never crossed my mind until right now that Ty might be somebody. Whatever that means. I didn't even know Ty existed until yesterday, but I guess that's the effect of doing stuff in the public eye. Diehards know everything, even session players apparently. He continues, "And I protect loyal customers. Like I said, family for me."

Now I'm anxious. "So . . . what is it?" I ask.

"What?"

"The thing Ty gave you for me."

"Oh, right. I don't know," he says. "Let me get it."

He goes in back, returns within seconds, and hands me a white envelope that has Christian written on it in black ink.

"What's your name?" I ask.

"Luis."

"Right! I remember now. Thanks, Luis."

"No worries. So, would you like a cup of coffee?" Luis asks.

"Black please."

"Go sit," he says. "I bring it over."

I sit at the same table as yesterday. I open the envelope and inside there's a handwritten note:

Christian,

Man, I had a feeling you would be back. I guess it means I didn't lay it on you too thick. I don't have much more to give you. I'm just an aging musician with a lot of mileage on these tires. The dots connected along the way, as they will with you, but you always gotta look at what's in front of you.

You know, people think people change, but that's bullshit. I seen a lot of people come and go over the years. People don't change; their interests change. Same person doing different stuff. Ain't nothing wrong with that either. Sure, you might lose some along the way, but you won't lose you. And that's the most important person not to lose.

I don't want to get all highbrow on you. I'm a just a fuckin' guitarist. Ha! Just don't kill yourself with consumption, kid. It's too easy to live a whole life creating nothing. I'll never tell you anything more important than that.

Enjoy the guitar pick. See you around.

Ty

PS - Let Luis know he's been making the coffee a tad hot lately.

I look in the envelope and there is a teardrop jazz pick with the initial T.W. Fuck, how cool it this? One of Ty's guitar picks.

I lift my head up, here comes Luis with my coffee and a newspaper under his left arm. "Here you are, amigo," he says.

"Ah, in a mug too," I say. "What a guy."

"Of course. Always a mug for family, amigo," he says. "I almost forgot Ty wanted me to give you this also." He hands me a copy of *The New York Times*.

"Thanks, Luis," I say and laugh to myself. "Oh, and one more thing. Ty says you've been making the coffee a tad too hot."

"What did you say, *pendejo*!?" he shouts. "I make the coffee at the perfect temperature every time! If he doesn't like it, he doesn't have to drink it!" He pauses, looks at me, and continues, "Next thing you're going to tell me is how to roast, too!?"

I sit there like I just saw a ghost. What fuck just happened?

"The door is right there," he says.

"I'm sorry . . . I was just . . . "

"I *never* make the coffee too hot," Luis says. "Ty's screwing with you."

"Phew, I was worried for a second," I say. Ty set me up. Luis starts laughing and I crack a smile.

"Go on," Luis says. "Enjoy your coffee."

I do just that, but find myself looking out the window more than reading the paper. I don't want to read the paper. I don't ever read. Fuck, I hate reading. It's torture. I only manage to flip through the pages, but there's something about the feeling of just sitting here that's unmistakable. Hard to explain, but quiet and different.

Still making an effort, I go to the sports section. This feels more intuitive, easy to read about the Yanks. I move along, flipping through the pages trying to find something of interest. Some things I read and others I pass over. The thing that seems to captivate me the most is the obituaries. Dead people. Obituaries make everyone sound important. So many lives, each one meaningful to someone out there.

I didn't notice it last time I was in here, but Sun's Up has no air conditioning. It's this sweltering morning that pulls that into focus. Even though it's hot as shit in here, the stillness enables me to hear, smell, taste, feel, and see everything.

It's sort of like the feeling I get when I'm with Liv. I can sense stuff deep in my core. Just like a footprint in the sand, things sink only where they need to, everything else just floats.

With a heightened sense of emotions, I begin to think about Liv. Is she what's in front of me? That's what Ty keeps saying, "Pay attention to what's in front of you."

Life is confusing, but love is good for a mushy brain. That I know. It gives you a high-voltage heart, electricity in your veins, and spark plugs for fingertips. Life starts to make sense. Maybe love is the moral center of your life. That's why you need it. I didn't want to fuck Liana, I didn't want to go to the strip club, shit, I just want to be different for Liv. I want her to see me as I see Ty, but I don't want to be Ty. It's the enamor I want to duplicate. Damn, this corner seat is powerful.

It's time I ask myself the question: What have I created?

Ty seems insistent on that. I take my own temperature

and come up hot. Very hot. It's obvious I haven't truly created much. I'm a consumer through and through—alcohol, women, drugs, bars, car, clothes, music, all consumed. Maybe I'm creating a career for myself, but am I really? I'm on the brink of disaster and verge of destruction. I'm teetering on throwing away seven years of service and successful track record. If I don't get my shit together, get strong, then it's possible. Why is love such a powerful drug?

I slip back into the real world when Luis greets a customer. A man in flip-flops buying coffees for an SUV full of people outside. I can hear Luis say, "Nice day out there, huh?"

"It is," the man says. "Heading up to Disney for a week."

"Enjoy, amigo."

I watch him walk out the door and jump back in the car. The people are grinning from ear to ear, coffees in hand, and like that they're gone.

I run my hand through my hair, rub my eyes, grab a napkin, and blow my nose. Cars zip by on the road. The shapes, colors, and models all seem to mess with my mind. They're all saying something to me. One says, "Don't be an idiot, Christian." Another says, "Fight for her, dummy." I give my head one good shake and open my eyes wide.

I swallow the last of my coffee, flip through *The Times* once more, and read an obituary. I signal to Luis. He sees me and asks, "Refill?"

"Yes please."

"One minute," he says. "I have to let it cool. It's a fresh pot."

SEVENTEEN

WHEN I GET BACK to the house, Tim is drinking coffee alone in the kitchen. His face is buried in his laptop screen while the TV plays news in the background. As soon as I walk toward him, he lifts his head, "Geez! You just scared the lights out of me."

"Sorry about that," I say.

"Where the heck were you?" he says. "I figured you were still knocked out sleeping."

"Oh, you know, just got some coffee. Couldn't sleep."

"Yeah, the booze will do that to you," he says. "Heck of a night last night. You having a good time?"

"Oh yeah," I say without hesitation. "That place was sick. Everything has been top-notch this weekend. I can't thank you enough."

"You don't have to thank me," he says. "You earned all of this. Where'd you get coffee?"

I pretend to not remember for a few seconds. "Hmm. Sun's Up I think it's called."

He smirks and says, "That little shithole? There's a Starbucks right down the road."

"It wasn't so bad," I say.

"Hey, whatever floats your boat," Tim says. "You haven't forgotten about what I told you, right?"

I actually have no idea what he is talking about. Damn booze. Oh, he is talking about the promotion. "How can I forget?" I tell him.

"Just making sure all those Tom Collins drinks don't damage your brain," he says. We share a brief laugh, then he continues, "We drank enough for a small village last night. I need you at full strength."

If only he knew the extent of it; last night was par for the course. My "great" work performance has always been conducted under a veil of consumption—consumption of booze, well, and other things.

"So, what was all that about having to leave last night?" I ask.

Tim picks his head up from the laptop. "That's what I'm doing now. I need to fly out this afternoon and I'm looking for flights."

"Yeah?"

"It's part of the gig. I wish I could stay, but if EP wants me there, I gotta be there," he says. "You get it."

I certainly do get it. It's part of being in the shit sandwich of management. What I don't understand is what that means for the rest of this trip.

"I do," I say. "So, do you want us to fly back with you then?"

"God no," he says. "You stay until tomorrow as planned. Go out in Miami, have some fun, enjoy yourself."

"Who's going to lock up the house?"

"Oh, don't worry about that. Olivia told me she's going to stay down here to lock up."

"Hmm, maybe I should just leave today," I say.

Tim stares at me. "Christian, if you leave I'll consider it an insult. I won't take no for an answer."

"Okay, okay."

This is not good. This development has trouble written all over it. I think about going to take a nap, to rest and gather myself. But I'm still a little on edge from the coffee earlier. Plus, the sun is calling my name.

"I think I'll go take a dip in the pool," I tell Tim.

With his head in the laptop, he says, "Have fun."

I head to my room and throw on my swim trunks. I don't want to go back through the kitchen and risk having more conversation, so I head to the pool through the sliding door in my bedroom. My mind is still on a wild goose chase from the experience this morning, and now Tim is leaving? Liv is going to be here alone?

I jump in, wade around, and do a few laps, then rest my back on the side facing the Intercoastal. What if I had gone to Starbucks instead of Sun's Up? Hm, I wonder. But meeting Ty was only a slight reprieve. A comforting moment for my wandering mind to escape the chaos.

Actually, I find a better Band-Aid. I slide my head under the water, hold my breath, and hide from my predicament.

I come up to the surface, twist my head wildly, feel my hair spin, and watch beads of water glide through the air then splash into the pool. Each drop creates the faintest ripple that subsides within seconds. I run my hands through my hair then take my index finger and thumb and run them down the sides of my nose. Ah, nothing like clearing your sinuses.

When I drift to the other side of the pool, there's a clear view of Undercuffler and Molly having coffee in the kitchen. Deeper in the background, I see someone else moving, coming into focus little by little. It's Liv. My heart skips a beat. Her hair is pulled back just like the first night I met her. I slide back under the water to take resolve from a scene that represents my immediate future—Undercuffler, Tim, and Liv.

When I come back up, Undercuffler is standing at the edge of the pool and looking at me. "I thought you weren't ever coming back up," he says. "I still can't get over those performers last night."

Undercuffler still stuck on the performers. Has he ever been out before? Ah, it was a good time, though.

"That place was rockin'," I tell him.

"You can say that again," he says. "So, I wanted to give you a heads-up, Molly and I are flying back this afternoon. I just talked to Tim. The little one has gotten sick, and since Tim is flying back, we figure we're going to call it, too. We're going to ride with him to the airport. Plus, it's going to rain tonight."

Now that his kiss-ass session with Tim is about to commence, he doesn't mind bailing. Typical Undercuffler.

"Oh really?" I say.

"Yeah, we just think it's best for the baby."

"No, I meant about the rain."

"Ha, you dick."

"Kidding," I say.

"Tim said that you and your butt buddy are going to ride it out."

"What did you say?"

He laughs. "That came out wrong. You and Jack are going to be staying 'til tomorrow."

I just nod my head and splash a little water on his leg.

"Oh, what the heck," he shouts. "I'm going to go pack!"

"Sounds good, buddy."

I dunk my head back under the water, before I have to

hear anything else, and the stillness surrounds me. I didn't know about the weather. Whatever, there's much worse than spending a rainy night in Miami. Tim's either lost in his own world or he really doesn't give a shit about Liv staying down here alone. Either way, the dominoes keep falling out of the way. As it appears, tonight will be Liv, Emma, Jack, and I, and the only danger is my bleeding heart. I'm a hazard only to myself. I'm just hoping I don't bleed out. This time when I come back up, I'm gasping for air, an instant reminder that even too much of a good thing can be damaging.

After catching my breath, I look up at the luminous house covered in sunlight, the same one purchased on the back of sorrow and darkness. A little girl had to die for it.

Jack comes fumbling out the sliders from my room wearing a tank top, pair of black mesh shorts, and nothing on his feet.

"Good thing we didn't go to the strip joint," he says, squinting through the sun. "I woke up hurt this morning." I splash some water on him. "Hey," he says. "I'm barely moving right now."

"I need to wake your ass up, sleeping beauty," I say. "We've got an escalating situation on our hands." He sits down on one of the pool chairs.

"What's that?"

"Everyone is leaving except Liv." That gets his eyes to open a little wider. "What?" he says. "What'd you do?"

"I didn't do anything, dude. Do you think I'd be floating here?"

"Well, what the hell is going on?"

"You don't remember what Tim said last night?" I ask him.

He's clueless. I proceed to tell him the situation—Tim got summoned, Undercuffler and Molly have to go play

Mom and Dad, so now we'll be here on our own with Liv, and Emma too.

"So, what does that mean for us?"

"Good question. I haven't thought that far yet."

I know I want to spend time with Liv, fuck it, what else would I do? Anyone would do the same thing, but I can't just come right out and say it to Jack.

"Well—last night in Miami, might as well do it up," he says. I don't respond. He continues, "Right?"

"Yeah, I mean, let's play it by ear," I say. "Your girl is still here, though."

"Who!?"

"Emma," I say, then laugh.

"Ahhh, ha, another night with her? I don't know, dude."

"You're an asshole," I say. Jack starts to crack a smile.

"Me? What about you!?" he shouts. "I'm over here with you in some weird fantasy land while you play hide and seek."

"Fantasy land?" I say.

He snaps back, "How was that jet ski ride yesterday, huh?"

I dunk my head under the water again. When I come up, Jack is sporting a devilish grin. "Why the delay, Christian? More hide-and-seek?"

Fuck this, I don't have to tell him shit, but this is what guys do, especially friends who've known each other for years. They pry and break balls.

"Do you really want to know?"

"I don't know. Do I?"

"She gave me a freakin' reach around, dude."

He starts to cackle louder than a hen in the morning. "Dude, you are so fucked," he says. "You just keep digging that grave further. You're almost six feet now. Soon, you'll just need a casket and a few nails."

Not exactly what I'm looking to hear, but I don't expect anything less from him. I can't tell him that it's more than just a physical attraction. He'd think I'm insane. I'm not about to go down that road with him until this thing with Liv plays itself out a little more. It's a total ego thing, some real macho bullshit that you can't escape growing up a guys' guy.

"You have no idea, dude," I whisper. "To make matters worse, Tim offered me a promotion, the guy under him is stepping down and he wants me to step in."

"What the . . . " he says. "What does that mean?"

"Well, more money, more responsibility, managing a team, basically another rung on the ladder. Oh, and more time with Tim."

"Christ, dude!" he says. "I've been in some hairy spots, but this one is pretty damn hairy."

"I know, I know."

"If I'm you, I abort the mission," he says. "ASAP."

I hop out of the pool, grab a towel from the rack tucked up against the house, and wonder what that even means—abort mission? Like he of all people should talk. I look into the kitchen and cross eyes with Liv. Damn it. Tim's still on his laptop with his back to me, meanwhile she's peering over his shoulder eyeing me up and down. Her look says, *I know we're going to be here alone tonight.* Those eyes are creating mini paper cuts all over my shirtless body. What the . . .

I escape the moment and look over my left shoulder to see Jack lying on the lounge chair with one leg hanging off and his left arm over his forehead.

"Hey buddy, you alright?"

He yells back, "I'm good. Just chillin'. Gotta be ready for tonight."

I look back into the kitchen and Tim is waving for me to come inside. Damn it. I open the sliding door. "What's up?"

He says, "Ah, it's already 11 and my flight leaves at 1. I just wanted to say goodbye."

"Wow—you're leaving already?"

"It was the best option. I have to leave now if I'm going to make it."

"I understand."

He gets up from the stool, walks over to me, shakes my hand, and pulls me in for a hug. "I had a great time. It sucks we have to cut it short, but enjoy the night. I'll see you back at the office," he says. "Big things on the horizon, my friend."

I can only respond, "Thanks, Tim. Get back safely."

"Oh, and tonight, while I'm gone, one rule . . . " he says to me. "Don't do anything I wouldn't do."

And that final request gives me a chill down to the bones.

EIGHTEEN

THE SOUND OF RAIN on the window could keep me dreaming all day. But something breaks the spell I'm under and my left eye starts to peel open. I flail on the bed and feel around as if I'm searching for lost keys, but all I grab is air. I'm not under the covers, either. I raise my head and there's a blurry shadow that needs to be put into focus. Like that, I'm hit with an uppercut that opens up my right eye. Liv is standing in the doorway.

"What are you doing?" I ask.

She responds, "You looked so peaceful I didn't want to wake you."

"You didn't answer my question," I say. "Let's try another. What time is it?"

"It's almost 5pm," she says with a smirk.

I can't believe I napped for that long. I shake out the cobwebs. "Where's Jack?"

"Not sure. I think he went shopping. He said something about not bringing enough clothes."

"And everyone else?"

"They left hours ago."

I'm here alone with Liv. A perfect manifestation of my desires is being gifted to me on a silver platter. The sight of her in yoga pants and bare feet makes little Christian starts to move. Fuck, I'm helpless.

"I bet you didn't expect this. You know . . . " Liv says. "Us being here . . . alone . . . together."

"You can say that," I say. "It's crazy that Tim had to go back."

She rolls her eyes.

"What?"

"You didn't really believe that?" she says. "Did you?"

"That he had to go back?"

"He's probably sleeping with the secretary again."

"Who? Lorelei?"

"It wouldn't be the first time."

What the. . . I rub my eyes. Again? I guess you never really know somebody. It doesn't surprise me. Late nights. Rocky relationship. Still, what an asshole.

"Not her," Liv continues. "It happened before he was at Perkins. I shouldn't have said it. He is still your boss."

"Don't remind me," I say with a smirk.

She cracks a smile, then just looks at me with her shoulder and head leaning on the doorframe. "Forget it," she says. "We're here now."

I consider asking more questions about Tim, but it doesn't matter. She's right. We're here now.

"Do you like it?" I ask her.

"Like what? Being here with you?"

I nod. "Yeah."

"Don't ask silly questions," she says.

"You didn't answer the question, you know?"

She smiles and shouts, "Of course! You're in my mind all the time." Hearing that provides quick electroshock treatment for my heart.

She continues, "Are you?"

I know what she's asking, but I like playing games so I ask, "Are I what?"

"Don't get all coy with me," she says. "Happy to be here alone with me?"

I'm undoubtedly enthused, but reluctant to say it aloud, so I murmur, "Yes."

"What!?"

"Yes Liv! Yes!" I say in a louder voice. "I feel something for you I haven't felt for anybody. There, are you happy I said it!?"

She giggles almost like she enjoys getting a rise out of me. "Whoa, pal! Take it easy."

I snicker. "Okay, that was a little abrupt, wasn't it?"

"Uh, yeah . . . but don't worry. I kinda liked it."

"So, what happened to never seeing each other again?" I ask.

"Well, technically we didn't, right?" she says. "We already knew we'd see each other here."

"That's true."

"Sometimes situations just present themselves and sometimes they're created," she says and pauses for a second. "I think ours just presented itself."

"Like on the jet ski yesterday," I say. "Just presented itself, right?"

She smiles. I can't help but smile back.

I'm sitting on the edge of the bed, Liv standing in the doorway, we just gaze at each other for a minute or two. The raindrops splashing on the window mirror my heart-beat. Pitter, patter, pitter, patter. Pump, pump, pump. Perfect synchrony.

"I want to take you somewhere," Liv says. "It's a five-minute walk."

"But it's raining."

"So? You've never walked in the rain before?" she asks.

Upon consideration, I never have actually walked in the rain. "I mean, I've got stuck in the rain, but I've never intentionally walked in the rain."

"Well, there's a first time for everything," she says. "It's only up the street. Plus, I have an umbrella." Her smile widens, then she continues, "C'mon. Let's go."

She's right, there is a first time for everything, and this whole situation feels like it's been dropped in via helicopter just for us to spend more time together. There's no shot I was ever going to say no.

"Let's go," I say.

She says, "I'll meet you at the front door," then turns away and I hear her voice trailing, "I'm going to throw something heavier on."

I hop out of bed and put on a zip-up hoodie. I go to meet Liv and she's waiting at the front door wearing a hoodie and a pair of oversized rubber rain boots. I look down at my flip-flops and she does too. I shrug and she laughs.

While holding the umbrella above our heads, we walk through what now feels like a gentle rain. It's more peaceful than I imagined—no wind gusts helps—but any time I open my mouth Liv cuts me off, "Shh . . . We're almost there." I don't push, and take her word for it.

She points. "You see, straight ahead?"

I squint to see a white stucco gate across the street that reads, "Town of Golden Beach Established 1929." There's not much traffic on the road. We cross over with ease.

"What is this place?"

"It's the town's beach park," she says.

"Beach park?"

"I don't know," she says. "That's what they call it."

"Oh, Miss Pissy Pants," I say. "Relax."

She stops us in her tracks, looks at me, and opens her eyes. "Well, I'm just saying."

In front of us stands a large white pavilion with pillars, arches, and a Spanish tile roof. It kind of reminds me of Jack's villa back home. It's open with some built-in tables underneath it. Not a soul is here. Liv and I walk under the pavilion as the rainfall starts to pick up. Good timing, I guess.

In the park, there's some covered outdoor furniture, white sand that's getting pounded with raindrops, and an empty lifeguard tower off to the right. Palm trees line the sides of the property and lead you into the Atlantic Ocean.

I drop the umbrella to our side, we look out toward the water with our hoodies fully zipped, covering our heads, and our hands stuffed into the kangaroo pockets.

"I wanted you to see this," Liv says.

I look at Liv while she stays focused on the water. I can see strands of blonde hair poking out of her hood and falling to either side of her face.

"On a nice day, it's probably amazing," I say.

Liv taps me on my shoulder. "I meant, I wanted you to see it now," she says. "I love coming here in the rain." She pauses for a moment. "It's just so quiet. Nobody comes here in the rain. It's this beautiful moment that everyone neglects. They run from it," Liv says. "Look at the ocean, it just goes and goes for miles, and the waves keep tumbling in. The rain falls on the surface and doesn't even affect it."

"The water gets rougher, though," I say.

"Sure, it gets rocky, but it just keeps moving along," she says. "I guess . . . I want to be more like the ocean."

This thought intrigues me, but there is just one thing I can't wrap my head around.

"Why would anyone want to stand in the rain if they didn't have to?" I ask.

She finally looks at me. "I think you're missing the point. It's not about wanting to stand in the rain, it's about not hiding from the rain, not being affected by it, because it's going to rain. It's always going to rain eventually."

I knew this would happen, damn it. It happens every time I'm alone with Liv, her aura pulls me into orbit. I get lost in her eyes while traveling through her mind. Completely enamored. It's the uninfluenced Liv that enthralls me, the Liv that lives inside Liv, that Liv illuminates through with natural sensibilities.

"You're beautiful. Do you know that?"

She giggles. "Don't flatter me."

"No, no I mean it. Not the way you look, but everything."

"I don't look beautiful?" Liv asks.

"Yes, *you're* beautiful, but it's the way you think, too. It's everything."

She smiles. "I know what you meant. I just wanted to hear you say it again."

I smack my head. "There it is again," I say. "Your beauty pops up in flashes!"

"Wait—so it's not always there?" she asks.

"You got me once," I say. "You're not going to get me again." She nudges me with her hand tucked into the end of her sweater sleeve.

"Cold?" I ask.

"Not really," she says. "I just always do this with my hands."

She taps my shoulder then grabs it and gives me two or three shakes.

"Are you alright?" I say.

"Sorry, I got excited. I thought of something. You know what would make this better?"

"Oh God. What?"

"The guitar!"

"Ah, yes. Music always adds to the moment," I say. "But it would kill your quietness."

"That would be worth it for me," she says. "You're really good, Christian."

Forget the guitar, it just feels good to be on her mind, even when I'm not with her. Maybe I thought that already, either way I like the reassurance.

"Well, you bring the best out of me."

"I already like you," she says. "You don't have to lie to me." I can't help but laugh.

"I'm not lying," I say with a big smile. "Anyway, I still can't get over that your favorite album is *Imagine*."

"Christian," she says. "I *love* that album."

"I know, I know."

Before Liv can get another word in about the album, I have an epiphany.

"Oh my God." I nudge her on the shoulder now.

"Geez. What is it?" she says.

"I almost forgot, I met Ty."

"No way, really? When?"

"It's crazy, I know," I say. "I met him at this little coffee shop."

"Sun's Up?"

"Yes! How'd you know?"

"Ty is always at that place," she says.

"Ha! Right, I found that out."

"He's kind of famous, you know," she says. "I mean, strangers know who he is, some strangers."

"I know. I found that out too," I say. "I can't believe you didn't tell me who he was. Not even that he played the guitar."

She scratches her head. "I didn't tell you any of that? I must have been distracted or something."

"What's the matter? Were you dazed and dazzled by a dashing young man?"

"Oh, please," she says. "Bewildered and hassled is more like it."

"Yeah, right, gimme a break."

"Joking," she says. "I guess I was a *little* distracted." I smile knowing that we are firing on all cylinders. Is there a better feeling in the world?

She continues, "Well, anyway, I'm happy you met him."

"Me too."

"I hope you got to talk with him for a little while."

"I did, I did," I tell her. "He . . . "

Somewhere in the middle of this exchange with Liv, I realize I don't want to divulge everything about the inter-action between me and Ty. For some strange reason, I want to keep it private. Undoubtedly, Liv thinks well of Ty, but I'm afraid that anything from her mouth might ruin the image I have of him in my head. I want him to be *that* person. I'd do the same for her. I'd protect her in my mind. It's the least you can do for someone you think highly of. You protect that image and relationship, or at least do what you can.

The sky begins to get darker, ocean tougher to see, our precious scene is coming to an end. We head back through rain before we lose any more sunlight with the umbrella over our heads. It gives us a sense of security. But how long will we have that?

It's about halfway back and I ask Liv, "Are you the ocean?"

She looks at me and tilts her head to the side. I begin to set the umbrella down. She says, "What are you doing!?"

"Being like the ocean, right?"

She smiles at me and nods. "Leave it."

We lie the umbrella on the road to wait for the next person who might need it. The rain pours on our heads without a care in the world, a neglected moment, that would be mine and Liv's forever. I'm not sure what is being held tighter: the grip of our hands or smile on our faces.

We arrive at the house, she fumbles the keys while I stand there observing her, just like two teenagers on their first date.

"Do you know the only thing that would make this better?" I say.

"What?"

"If I kissed you."

"Well, kiss me," she says.

So, while raindrops continue soaking our hair and running on our faces, we share the most cliché kiss of all time. But you know? It lives up to the hype. It's a delicate and fragile exchange of honesty. Pure, like the Virgin Mary. A kiss that will linger for eternity. At least in my mind.

We step through the doorway, I flick on the light, and almost instantly I hear a banging noise. Liv and I look at each other wet and shivering, and, for a moment, we both think the worst. Tim?

The sound is coming from across the house. I squint and see someone banging on the glass doors that open to the pool. Holy shit, it's Jack. I run through the house soaking wet and open the sliding door.

"I tried texting you. Calling you, nothing," he yells. "Where the fuck have you been?"

I feel around in my pockets, front, back, sweatshirt, and come up empty. "Shit, I must have left my phone here," I say. "I thought you were with Emma."

"I took an Uber back here because Emma wanted to

keep shopping," he says. "I've just been standing back here under the overhang for 20 minutes!"

"Sorry, dude," I say. "We went out."

"Out? It's pouring!" he says. "Sorry, dude? That's it. While you two fuckers are off doing God knows what, I've been standing here getting drenched!"

"Oh, relax," I say. "It's just rain."

"Right, just rain," he says. "Rain that soaked the new clothes I just bought."

Jack reaches down, lifts a shopping bag up in the air, and we watch water drip from the bottom. I look back at Liv, she looks back at me, and we just laugh.

———

Evening comes and Jack is pleading for us to go scorch ourselves in the heat of Miami nightlife. After much hemming and hawing, he doesn't win out: there isn't a snowball's chance in hell I'm going to waste this opportunity staring at Jack's drunken face. I have the woman I want to spend time with right in front of me. Plus, our flights leave early tomorrow morning. We decide——correction——I decide to keep the night low-key and grab dinner with the girls. Jack is reluctantly coming along, but after a few drinks I know his sourpuss will simmer and subside. Sorry, bud. I don't have much room for anything else in my mind than what to do about Liv. I mean, tonight will last only for tonight——then what? What will she want to do about me? What are *we* going to do?

I tell Liv I want to chat with her before we go out. I think she knows what is coming, a conversation about our future. There's a hesitance in her voice and slight discomfort in her tone. When push comes to shove, I can't be sure how the conversation will go, but I know how the night will go. The night will be a good time and I didn't want to risk ruining that. Sales 101: always handle the objections first so the rest of the sales call is a gradual build. Tough conversations are, well, tough. Mainly because people will say anything in the moment just to get through them. Myself included. Do people *really* mean what they say? I don't know, that's the call you have to make.

Jack is getting ready and Emma hasn't made it to the house yet. I arrive in the kitchen before Liv, so I take the liberty of mixing myself a Tom Collins. I look around at the empty house, faintly hear music coming from upstairs, and I wonder how I got here. It's easy for me to connect the dots and make sense of the chance encounters that shaped this situation, but it doesn't change the fact that I'm here now.

Maybe Ty is right when he says, "The dots connected along the way, as they will with you." Thinking of him brings me back to my first and only real conversation with him. "We always want what we can't have," seemed to be a throwaway line, but right now it feels more pertinent than ever. Maybe having skin in the game does change everything. How you feel? How you see? How you think? How you do? Is the idea of Liv better than Liv? It all seems to not matter when I'm face-to-face with her, rational thoughts are kites on a windy day, drifting and floating away.

I hear the buzzing sound of music go silent and footsteps begin to march along the ceiling above me, resembling a countdown timer on my future. I watch the rain splatter the surface of the otherwise still pool, sip my drink, and wait patiently, lost in thought. Hints of florals and spices begin to tickle my nose. Maybe a touch of creamy vanilla. I know that smell. I know Liv is behind me before she can say, "Earth to Christian."

I turn around and she's dressed in similar attire to the last night we spent together. That air of edginess about her displayed by the rips in her jeans, heeled boots, waves in her hair, and oversized cropped shirt. It isn't her shoulders shooting flames tonight, it's the bare skin of her stomach I catch a glimpse of when she raises her arm. And, of course, her emeralds for eyes.

I probably could have used the time alone or thought more about exactly what I want, but who does that? Now I struggle to open the conversation and I'm left with the first thing that comes to my mind.

"You knew this conversation was coming, didn't you?" I ask.

"Am I going to need a drink?"

"Plenty of time for that later," I say. "You know how I feel about you, right?"

She nods.

I place my drink down on the kitchen island, move closer to Liv, and sit on the stool. "Well, I've been at such odds with myself over what to do about us," I say. "Obviously the situation is pretty complicated. Plus, I don't know where you stand. I mean, I don't even have your number."

"I know, Christian," she says. "It's so complicated."

Our eyes are locked, not even a blink, and I'm trying to see into her mind, but I have to just own up to what I feel, and say it.

"I can't help but want to spend more time with you. I want to go on actual dates, not have to sneak around, or worry about who's going to say what about what. I want to listen to music with you, I want to do that more than anything."

"Don't make me cry, Christian."

I pause for a moment, grab her hand, and continue,

"Play the guitar for you, walk in the rain with you, and I don't know . . . just be with you."

She tucks her top lip under her bottom one and grabs my other hand. "I'd be lying to you if I said I didn't want that too," she says. "You create an electricity inside me that lasts a day, week sometimes, and it's true, my marriage has been on the rocks since the tragedy of my daughter, but . . . " She pauses for a moment; my heart begins to sink.

"But even if I was to end things with Tim, I can't ask you to throw away your career for me. It's your life. What about your job? Your future?"

She has a valid point and she probably doesn't even know about the promotion. There's no way to escape the obvious. I feel as though I'm being waterboarded and, with each admission of my feelings, the torture slows little by little. The vulnerability rises, but the weight reduces. Fuck it, I might as well keep going.

"I don't know what I'll do, Liv. I know I'll have to come clean to Tim and let the cards fall as they may. The only other option is to continue the same way, but how can we do *that*? I have to work with Tim every day. How long can that boat stay afloat? Honestly." I squeeze her hands. "It just seems so wrong. Dangerous. It just brushes the problem under the rug, not sweep it up."

I pause again because I know the question I have to ask. I need to dig deep to get it out, but it has to be said right now, at this moment. I just go for it and muster out, "I mean, do you want to be with me?"

Her eyes are starting to swell, and the moisture builds between our palms. I feel that electricity shooting out of her fingertips as they dig into the backside of my hand. The tension breaks.

"I do, Christian," she says, then wipes a single tear that's fallen from her right eye. "I just need some time to talk to Tim. I've got to have the conversation first. The D conversation. Can you give me some time?"

I feel something I haven't felt since I was a kid playing little league baseball. A sense of relief, similar to hitting my first home run. It is ecstasy.

I'm reluctant to say, "Of course, I can give you time," but I have no choice, so I do. Then I continue, "It'll be good for me to gather my thoughts too. I should be prepared for whatever comes my way. Just when the time is right, let me tell Tim about us. I can't have that bomb drop on me at the office."

She nods, then pulls me in closer, throws her arms around my body, and rests her head on my left shoulder. We stand there with no movement for the next three minutes which feels more like three hours. She leans back in, and places her soft lips on mine, pulls back again, and looks at me.

"I guess this means I should give you my number now," she says.

I smile. "Probably."

"Actually, give me *your* number," she says. "After I talk to Tim, then I'll contact you. Last thing I need is for you to call or text me while I'm with him, raise a red flag prematurely, and him to get suspicious. Will that work for you?"

"That's smart," I say. "And perfect."

"Let's not tell Tweedle Dee and Tweedle Dum, and just enjoy the night," she says.

She smiles, bites her bottom lip, and waits for confirmation.

"Good idea," I tell her.

"Now I need to go freshen up," she says. "You ruined my makeup!" Then she strides off toward the staircase.

I laugh. "Oh really?"

She yells back with some sass, "Hey, you wanted me,

now you got me. Wait, how did you say it? You fucked me and fought for me—is that how it goes?"

I laugh to myself about the absurdity of that comment. I can't even believe that I said it, not once, but twice. It sounds so ridiculous now, but I guess there is an element of truth to it.

I pick up my Tom Collins, swirl it around, and take a gulp. The ice bumps my upper lip and reminds me of how cold reality can be. I will enjoy the night while knowing there are still many chilly conversations that live in my future.

NINETEEN

WE BARELY MADE IT back to the house. And, similar to the
first time we made love, Liv and I are in a liquefied haze.
There's nothing gentle about it. The only thing louder
than the sound of Liv's voice saying my name is the sound
of her heart up against me. It's pounding the bass line
from 'Come Together,' which is fitting because that's
exactly what we're doing.

I can see the shimmer on our skin from perspiration
making our movements frictionless. It's not glue holding us
together, we're working hard to stay this close. But we are
meant to be here, on a bed with no comforter and soft
linen sheets, and sweat dripping from our bodies. I can see
Liv reach down to grab me, stroke after stroke, the bed
rocks, and a voice gets louder and louder and louder.

That voice gets deeper and I start to get confused.
Until it's not, "Christian, Christian" in my head anymore .
. . it's, "Ballantine, Ballantine."

"Hello, anyone home!?" the voice says. It sounds more
like . . . Undercuffler? Then I feel a literal nudge on my
shoulder.

I give my head one good shake and, all at once, I snap out of it.

Undercuffler is standing next to me in the office and I'm sitting at my desk. "I don't know what kind of drugs you're taking," he says. "But you have been out of it since you got back from Florida."

"I've just been struggling to get back into the flow of things," I say.

"Well, you better start soon," he says. "I bumped into Tim this morning and he told me if I saw you to let you know he's trying to get ahold of you and that he's still waiting on a reply to an email he said he sent you."

"Shit, thanks man."

He laughs. "Get it together, will ya."

It's Friday morning and I've been on pins and needles all week. Every damn day I wonder if today's going to be the day I walk into work and Tim wants to chop my head off. Plus, I haven't heard from Liv. All I can do is daydream about our last night together. Maybe Tom Petty is right? The waiting *is* the hardest part.

It was mid-afternoon on Wednesday when I realized this scenario might play itself out—not hearing from Liv yet, but still having to give Tim a response on the promotion. I don't see much sense in denying it. When the time is right, I'll just accept the promotion, and roll the dice. Sure, middle management is brutal. I'd rather be in those shoes when the hammer drops. I don't have to tell him right away. I'm sure many homewreckers or philanderers have used this strategy. I can assume the new role for a while and let some time pass. Harder to do anything crazy and lessen the sting. Well, that's the plan anyway.

The damn promotion conversation is coming sooner than I thought. Olson hasn't mentioned anything to me, but I know they're planning to announce him leaving soon.

Next week maybe. I start to go through old emails, they've been building up all week so there are more than a few. Ah, the one from Tim. Wow—it was sent last night. Not terrible, I guess.

Lunch tomorrow, noon at Max's? Couple of updates for you. Need to chat. - Tim

I can tell him I can't make it, but that's just delaying the inevitable. If he truly needs to talk then he's going to get ahold of me one way or another. Plus, I've already made the decision that I'll just accept the promotion. Maybe I don't want to be the shit in the shit sandwich that is management, but I know I deserve it. And just thinking about having a conversation with Undercuffler as my boss gives me indigestion. So, I email Tim back, "Sorry for the delay. Tied up all morning. See you at noon!"

He emails back instantly, "See you then." I'm not worried about the short answers, executives are notorious for sending short responses, after all they're really "busy." But I'm worried about how fast he replied. Was he sitting there waiting on me? I don't want to think about it. Either way, I'm going to meet him. At least Max's makes a great burger. I try to look forward to that.

It's a beautiful spring day, clear skies, high 60s or low 70s depending on who you ask. The city has a little extra buzz today, not that it's ever slow, but on days like this, people want to walk around rather than have to walk around. With such nice weather and a comfortable pair of loafers on my feet, I stroll the three blocks up to Max's.

You can see every type of person imaginable on a walk in Manhattan. It's America summed up in five minutes, a melting pot of people completed with honking horns, flashing lights, and the occasional, "Ah, screw you!" thrown in for good measure.

Before I realize it, I arrive at Max's. The maître d' greets me, "Hello Sir, do you have a reservation?"

"It's probably under Tim. For two," I say. He starts to scroll the reservation list.

"Ah, here it is. The other party is already here. Right this way, Sir. Follow me."

The place is packed, typical for a Friday and similar to the Metro-North train in the morning Max's is full of costumes—people trying to impress, feel important, and be somebody. The lunch and dinner crowd throughout the week is what keeps these places in business. It's all company men with overblown expense accounts. Everyone plays the game, so nobody blinks an eye at the $20 burger. That's the lowest priced item on the menu. I've seen dinner bills for four get into the $3,000-$4,000 range. It's the "I appreciate or want your business" wine that raises the bill to astronomical figures. But nobody gives a shit, they're not paying for it, the company is. It's a well-oiled machine, people are the oil, restaurants and businesses are the parts, and Manhattan is the machine.

I spot Tim, he's sitting up in the back corner and already looking my way. The maître d' moves to the side once we reach the table, extends his left arm, and says, "Here you are, Sir."

I thank him and take a seat.

"I thought you ran away," Tim says as soon as I sit down.

"Ran away?" I'm a bit confused, it seems like a strange way to start a conversation.

"Well, I haven't heard much from you since we got back, and typically you respond quickly to emails."

Ahh, now I see where he's going with this, but still no hello, good to see you, or anything. "I just been struggling to get back into the workflow," I say. "I'll be back to my normal self by Monday."

He looks at the menu, then back up at me. He says, "I thought I'd hear back from you much sooner on what we had discussed in Florida." Then goes back to looking at the menu.

"I ended up needing a little time to think about it."

"Yeah, but still, it's been crickets," he says. "Very unlike you, Christian. You know, not even anything about the trip."

Fuck, did I forget to thank him? Maybe I did. I definitely did. I can feel my palms getting sweaty. Am I about to walk into an ambush?

"The trip was great, Tim. I had a great time. I can't thank you enough."

"I'm glad you had a good time." he says. "About the promotion, I thought you'd be honored to take it. Undercuffler wouldn't have needed more than two minutes."

The waiter arrives before I can respond. "Would you like anything to drink?" he asks us. Tim looks at me, I don't say a word, and just wait for his lead.

"You know what, it's Friday. Bring each of us a Tom Collins," he says. "And ask the bartender to use one sugar cube rather than simple syrup."

"Well, someone knows how they want their drink," the waiter says. "You got it."

Sugar cube? He didn't even know what the hell a Tom Collins even was before last Friday.

"So, I inspired you, huh?" I smile. "I didn't even see you drink a Tom Collins in Florida." I'm hoping to get a little chuckle out of him or something.

"Oh yeah. Club soda, lemon juice, gin, and one sugar cube. I had my first one last night actually."

"Happy to have you on the team." I smile. Tim's face is still flat.

"Yeah. I was at this little spot in Connecticut," he says. "Fatty Duck, have you ever been?"

What did he just say? I choke on my water and squeeze my butt cheeks together. He's either setting me up or it's pure coincidence. Too early to call. Maybe I should have worn socks today. I can feel my bare feet sticking to my loafers.

"Excuse me," I say, wiping my mouth. "Must have swallowed wrong. I have been to Fatty Duck. It's a good little spot."

Tim puts the menu down. "So, it was the craziest thing . . . " he says. "I was meeting a friend for dinner who lives in Connecticut and he suggested we go there. I'd never been."

"That doesn't sound so crazy to me," I say. I cut him off, which probably isn't a good idea, but the nerves are making my mouth jumpy.

He raises his right index finger and says, "Wait—we haven't got to the crazy part yet." I take another sip of water, trying to stay cool.

Tim continues, "So, as I was saying . . . I'm sitting at the bar with my buddy and the bartender asks me what I'll have." Tim leans in looking me straight in the eye. "And this is where it gets good," he says.

I notice my grip on the water glass is getting tighter. I try to keep playing it cool and don't move.

"So, I'm at the bar and I think of the trip, you and

your silly drink, and everything on the horizon at work. So, I tell her, 'You know *what*, I'll have a Tom Collins.' She laughs when I say this. So, I ask her, 'What's so funny?' And she answers, '*Nobody* orders that drink anymore, except one young guy who's been in here a couple times.' A good bartender never forgets, she tells me."

Fuck, fuck, fuck.

"'I know a young guy who drinks those all the time too' I tell her," he says. "I don't know why I asked what I asked next, but I did and let me tell you, Christian, am I happy that I did."

"What did you ask her?"

"I asked her, 'What does he look like?' And she goes on to describe you verbatim. And I was so excited because I'm like, what are the chances? So, I tell her, 'It's *gotta* be my friend and coworker Christian. He drinks these damn things all the time.'"

"Wow—what are the odds? Pretty crazy."

Tim raises that same right index finger again. "No, no it gets even *crazier*," he tells me.

"The bartender does what most bartenders do, especially on a slow night, she keeps chatting with me. 'Yup, I remember vividly both times he was with the same woman, too' and she goes on to describe her, 'unmistakable green eyes, blonde hair, pointy shoulders, a little older,' and on and on and on."

The story comes to a standstill as the waiter comes back with a Tom Collins in each hand, and I can feel my face starting to get flush. I subtly place my hand between my legs to make sure I haven't peed myself.

"Grab your drink," Tim says. "I want to make a toast."

My hand shakes as I pick up my drink and raise it.

"Here's to all things we love," he says. "And to all things we've lost."

We clink glasses and both take a sip.

"Ah, good isn't it?" Tim asks me with a huge smile.

Just drop the hammer, dude. Drop the effin' hammer.

"Yeah, good," I say. "Definitely well-crafted."

He positions his glass back on the table. "So, where was I?" he asks. "Do you remember?" He's fucking me with now.

"Ah . . . I believe . . . the woman or something."

"Oh yes, of course, the woman," he says. "As she's telling me all this, I think, 'That sounds an awful lot like Olivia. No, it can't be, can it?' So, you can imagine I was a little perplexed, but why would it be my wife? I stopped thinking about it. But after a few more drinks, it hit me."

"What's that, Tim?" I ask, trying to hold my composure.

"A few weeks back, Olivia went to dinner with Emma somewhere in Connecticut. I couldn't remember for the life me the name of the place, so I scrolled back in my text messages with her and, sure enough, they went to the Fatty Duck!"

Now I'm full-on sweating. Palms, underarms, it's all damp. I'm thinking, only answer questions that he asks you, nothing more, nothing less. Sit here and keep your mouth shut.

"So, here's where it gets *really* crazy . . . " Tim continues. "Do you know why I was out with my friend that night, Christian?"

Okay that's a question, I have to answer. "I don't, Tim."

"I was out with my friend because on Wednesday Olivia told me she wants to separate. Things have been rocky, but it was still a blow. I didn't see it coming. So, when I told my buddy, he said we should go out for some drinks. Now here I am, hurting, wheels spinning, all this info, and I start to retrace some steps. Then I remember the first night in Golden Beach, you called her Liv, and your dumb-ass friend tells us his name is Jackson and you call people nicknames all the time. It was off, but I still think there's no way. Just no fucking way."

He pauses, lifts up that index finger again, and says, "Then I get to thinking *even* more, and I remember when I told Olivia to pick up gin and lemon juice, she asked about *sugar?* I laughed it off after she made up some lame excuse that I believed. But now I'm sitting here thinking, 'If they did know each other, why wouldn't they just tell me? Even if they just bumped into each other, why wouldn't they say so? It would make for a great story . . . '"

He takes another sip of his drink, looks out the window, and back at my hollow face. "Now are you ready for the really, really crazy part?" he asks. "C'mon, Christian, tell me you're ready."

Fuck, that's another question.

"Uh-huh," is all I can manage, even though it's not true. I sit there squeamishly, waiting to take it like an anvil. This is going to be painful, but what choice do I have?

"So, the wheels were spinning when I got home. Olivia was already sleeping so I didn't bother waking her up, but I think, 'Let me check the security cameras I have at the Golden Beach house.' A neighbor told me to install them at all the entrances since I'm not there all the time. It's amazing, Christian, these tapes keep footage for a year," he tells me. "What do you know? The night I left to come back to New York, I see you and Olivia go prancing out the front door in the rain under one umbrella. That's odd, so I fast forward a bit and see Jack banging on the door, then going around back trying to see if the sliders are open. So, I fast forward just a little more . . . and there it is."

I know exactly what he saw, how could I forget that kiss in the rain? It is imprinted in my mind forever and, apparently, on film as well.

Tim continues, "It's too bad you didn't leave the umbrella up. It would have made it harder to tell what you were doing. But, nope, there you two are, holding hands and smacking lips in the rain. And, of course, later that night all four of you go out and you and Olivia come back in the house together at the wee hours of the morning. God only knows what you did after that."

"Tim, I'm . . . " I begin to say.

"Save it," he says in a much louder tone. "I'm going to ask you this one time. Have you been sleeping with my wife?"

Shit, that's definitely another question, the one I've been dreading since this whole thing started. If it's going to come to this, I want to get ahead of it, but here I am caught with my tail between my legs.

I only have two options: admit or deny. If I deny, then I really look like a shitbag. I kissed his wife *after* he handed me an award, brought me into his home, and offered me a promotion. If I admit, then I can at least tell the truth, maybe he'll understand the predicament I was in all along. The decision seems easy to me. So, I own it.

"Yes," I tell him.

Tim's eyes don't even widen, move, or blink. It's like he already knew the answer was coming.

"You dumb fuck," he says. "Is that all you're going to say?"

Okay, that's definitely another question. I should just answer yes or no, but, after all, this might be my only opportunity to speak my piece. I break my own rule and elaborate.

"Tim, I know you're livid, but hear me out," I say.

"When I first met Liv, Olivia, whatever you want me to call her. I'm sorry. When I met her, I had no clue she was your wife. I only found out at the awards dinner. I thought if I didn't say anything it would just go away. I could continue along with my career and life, but then this happened."

"There's eight million people in this city, and you had to pick my wife," he says. "My fucking wife?"

"I know, Tim," I say. "It looks really bad."

"Looks really bad?" he repeats. "If you're so innocent, let me ask you: did you see her again after you knew? After the awards dinner?"

Oh boy. The yarn is officially unraveling, and I know deep inside that there will be no coming back from this. I can barely get the words out of my mouth.

"I did," I say.

"All you had to do was come to me like a fucking man after the first time," he shouts. "Instead you saw her again?"

He is right and I am speechless. What can I say? I love her, but what good will that do? She's his wife.

"You know who Friedrich Nietzsche is?" Tim goes on, "Actually, I don't give a shit if you know who he is or not. He once wrote, 'I'm not upset that you lied to me, I'm upset that from now on I can't believe you.'"

There's nothing for me to say. I have to be the whipping post. Offering any details will do more harm than good. All I can do is look at the disappointment that runs from Tim's forehead wrinkles down to his clenched jaw.

"The promotion is gone," he says. "Now it makes sense why you were delaying. You had the world at your fingertips. You threw it all away—for what? A piece of ass. Do you even know what Olivia and I have been through? Do you even understand what a marriage is!?"

I know I don't have to answer, but it is that last set of rhetorical questions that makes me blow my lid.

"Tim," I say. "I got to know her, she got to know me, and I fell in love with her. That's why I couldn't resist her again in Golden Beach."

Tim's inner bull makes his ears steam, he leans forward ready to charge, eyes full of rage, but he grips the corners of the table to hold himself back. "Enough!" he yells.

All eyes are now on our table. People start to notice something isn't right. He adjusts himself, pulls down the sleeves on his sports coat, and gathers himself.

"Listen here. You have two choices. One: you stop seeing Olivia and you might be able to keep your job *or* two: you're done at Perkins, fired today. But I'm a nice guy, Christian, as a courtesy I'll let you write a resignation letter, consider it your new promotion offer. Rather than getting fired, you can resign. So, what will it be?" he asks. "Option one or option two?"

Fired? Fuck, my entire life flashes before my eyes. I can hear my Father say, "Just like when you quit baseball, Christian. You really screwed this one up." My Mother just shakes her head, not knowing what to say. Jacob calls me a dumb-ass and asks, "How do you plan on paying for that expensive car?" And Jack says, "I told you so!"

The thought of Undercuffler being my new boss and Olson handing him the keys to his office is giving me a gag reflex. What would Ty do? All I can hear is him saying, "Don't kill yourself with consumption, kid."

"Time is ticking," Tim says. "Don't be a dumb-ass, Christian."

As soon as he says that, everything slows down and I can see Liv. Her emerald eyes burning a hole in my soul, sitting barefoot on my couch, and standing in the rain. The feeling of her soft skin tenderizes the rigidness of the moment. It's the depth of her senses that washes away every other thought.

It's hard to look at him. "I can't stop seeing her," I say with my head hanging.

He just shakes his head, possibly defeated, probably disgusted.

"Don't bother coming back to the office," he says. "Email your resignation letter by the end of the day."

He gets up, buttons his suit jacket, throws a hundred-dollar bill on the table, and says, "The drinks are on me. I owe Tom one."

I sit there, looking at the empty chair and wrinkled hundred on the table, and wonder if people are whispering about me. The hustle and bustle of New York City keeps moving along outside the window. The breadth and impact of losing my job has not begun to set in yet. Maybe the smart move would have been to stop seeing Liv, but that would be like removing a limb. How can I remove a limb?

I look down and stare at my Tom Collins. The club soda is bubbling while the lemon wedge shines bright. This one is garnished with a cherry on top. Go figure. The gin and sugar are invisible, waiting to bite only once you taste it. So I take a sip just to remind me.

TWENTY

IT'S BEEN ONE WEEK since my conversation with Tim, and I haven't left my bed since. I've avoided all contact with humans, thinking once I'm not tangled in a web of uncertainty, maybe it'll be easier to break the news to the people closest to me. I'm hoping this story has a good ending, but I haven't heard from Liv yet. And each day that passes makes the odds feel like they're getting worse and worse. The only time I get out of bed is to piss, shit, eat, or wash. The last of the four I've done sparingly. What's the difference? I can't smell my own body odor anyway.

My life is hanging in the balance and it's making me think too much about everything I do. Just whether to leave the house gets questioned. Why? I could just watch another episode of whatever the fuck I'm watching. It's easier, that's for sure. Or I could just eat another peanut butter and jelly sandwich. Shit, I have no more bread. Do I have to leave the house? Fuck it, I'll just use some crackers instead.

I'm frozen in time, every movie triggers the voices in my head, and any song makes my eyes water. Even playing with myself is a risk to my emotional state. I pick up the guitar a few times, but my hands feel like stones and it only reminds me of her. So, I put it down as fast as I picked it up. I watch *Aladdin* and the rest of the day I keep staring at my sock drawer, waiting and wishing for the genie to pop out and grant me three wishes. I try to listen to *Imagine* a few times, but can't even get through the album once. That's possibly the worst thing I did. I can smell her. Taste her. Feel her. And I keep wondering why I still haven't heard from Liv. Where is she? What is she doing? Why hasn't she texted me?

I do hear from my parents about coming for dinner on Sunday, but not even that can get me out of the house. I text them that I can't make it. They are probably disappointed, but that's nothing compared to the disappointment they'll have when they find out what happened. I see a message from my brother Jacob, too. Something about me having to come visit him on the other coast. I tell him things are too busy right now. My whole family dynamic is out of whack, I'm supposed to be the one with my shit together, not falling apart. What do I even tell them all? I threw away my six-figure job because I was fucking the boss's wife and fell in love with her. It sounds like a damn fairy tale. Nobody would even believe that.

Jack is the only one who I almost reach out to. He tries to contact me a bunch over the weekend, but all I can do is text him, "I'm tied up." I need some consoling, not someone fucking with me. He'd just tell me he warned me and now let's go make the most of that free time. Maybe he'd be right, but right now I can't hack it. I know he has Emma's number, so that would be a way to possibly contact Liv, but she told me to wait for her. I just want to send a smoke signal, "Hey, I'm alive? Do you remember me?"

After I draw up my resignation letter, I get calls and

voicemails from coworkers all wanting to know why I left, how it happened, and where I was going. Undercuffler and Olson are more concerned than their usual dick selves. Olson even uses the term, "You were at the top of the mountain," a phrase that cuts straight through my wounded skin and spikes my nervous system. They'll all find out eventually, these things find their way through an office, God bless Tim. Poor guy. It's not the easiest situation to navigate. It's best to not answer anyone and let the dust settle. I don't have the guts to answer anyway.

Dear Mr. Alexander,

Please accept this letter as notice that I will be resigning from my job at Perkins LP effective immediately. I will be moving on to explore different interests and opportunities.

Thank you for the support and opportunities that you've provided me throughout my employment. If there is anything I can do to help the transition in finding a replacement, please let me know.

Sincerely,

Christian Ballantine

The resignation letter is simple and nondescript. A bunch of times, I think about the legality around Tim forcing my hand. Sure, I could have sued or put up a fight—maybe I should have. But the truth of the matter is: I deserved it. Plus, if I managed to stay, what would that have been like? Tim still would be my boss. How could I work like that every day? The flubs would be ordeals, and wins would be worthless. Just a ticking time bomb, really. What's done is done.

So here I lie in a malaise thicker than a dense fog. Lovesick. The minutes and days blend together, but there's a first time for everything, I guess. The lone spots of happiness are the memories of the time spent with Liv and the hope that we have more moments in the near future. I threw away my job in the name of love.

In between daydreams, I hear a knock on the door. I can't distinguish whether it's an actual knock or a random noise coming from the TV. I prop myself up a little and listen, but don't hear anything. I stare back at the TV and watch lions hunt their prey in the African safari. Definitely no knocking there. But just the thought of someone at my door gives me anxiety. Nobody would expect me home on a Friday midday. Maybe I'm just hearing things. Fuck, am I losing it?

A little time passes, but the possibility is driving me insane. I pry myself from the sheets and lumber into the living room. The sun is blazing through the open blinds, you can see a thin layer of dust covering everything in the room, and once my eyes hit the door, they scan down to the ground. There's an envelope on the floor.

I walk over, look out the peephole, and see nobody. My back creaks as I bend down to pick up the envelope. Still curious, I open the door, poke my head out, look up and down the hallway, and nobody. While turning toward the couch, I release the doorknob from my grasp, and allow gravity to slam the door shut. I plop myself down on the sofa and look at the envelope. Handwritten and underlined in black sharpie, all it says is, "Christian." I open it and inside there's a note.

Christian,

I'm sorry it took me so long to contact you. I'm writing to let you know that right now we can't be together. I owe it to both myself and Tim to work on our marriage. He doesn't know I'm writing this letter

to you, but I owe that to you. At least that, but I know you'll
understand.

Tim and I have been through things that most marriages never
have to go through. When Chloe passed, there was a lot of rain, I
tried to hide from it and Tim tried to mask it with the house, among
other things. This is my shot at being like the ocean.

Sometimes people flash into your life like a shooting star and
remind you of all the possibilities that exist. You did that for me,
Christian. The moments we had together were real, so real that you
reminded me of who I was, who I am, and who I want to be. You've
changed me forever.

I'm so sorry to hear about work, but the Christian I know will
find his way. Maybe in the future we'll meet again under different
circumstances. You'll always be in my heart.

XO,
Liv
PS - Never lose that playfulness, life is too hard.

A stake through my heart. Every morsel of hope evapo-
rates right before my eyes. I do all I can to hold the tears
back, but I let one or two drip on the letter and some of
the black ink runs down the page. I use the pillows on the
couch to wipe my face. I think about drinking to ease the
pain, maybe even calling Handley, but I just end up sitting
in the same spot motionless for the next two hours.

Should I fight for her? That's the question I keep
asking myself over and over. I still have to respect her
wishes, even if I feel in my heart that Liv should be with
me, she went from separated and looking for a fresh start
to a married woman working on her marriage. How can I
disrupt that? I can't. How foolish am I to think I can just
waltz in and steal her away from a ten-year marriage? Did
I honestly think this was ever going to end with rainbows

and sunshine? I guess I did. I scream into a pillow, "Liiii-iiiiiiv!"

Wait—is she the one who slid the letter under my door? She was right there and the only thing separating us was a locked door.

Fuck, it doesn't even matter.

She doesn't need to say why she wrote the letter rather than text me or why she doesn't orchestrate some face-to-face. I know it's better that I don't have her number or any way of contacting her. Sure, I wish I got to see her once more, but I know that having this conversation in person is just not possible. Fuck me.

All those visions of white chariots, one-on-one concerts, and life-changing sunsets abolished with one letter. No more jet ski rides or ice cream in the cold weather. At least I have plenty of rain to walk in. Damn it, Christian.

The emptiness of my apartment reminds me that I'm alone and the loneliness is only compounded by the letter in my hand. The harsh reality of being womanless and jobless starts to sink in. Finding a new gig isn't really bothering me as much as it probably should be, though. Selling organizations are always looking for salespeople with a good track record, and that is something I have. I don't know what the future holds, but I know it's Liv-less. That makes me cry some more. I feel like someone ripped my heart out, smashed it with a meat tenderizer until it resembled a piece of jerky, then gave it back to me and said, "Here you go, you'll be fine, go live the rest of your life."

Now I'm really screwed on what to tell everyone. Liv was my fallback, the escape net that allowed me to jump out the back window, and ride off into the countryside. Last week, I was the golden goose and this week I'm the golden dipshit.

I've been in the same position, sunk into the couch, and legs perched on the coffee table for so long that there's indents on my calves and I can't feel my feet. And my ass is numb. I let out a sigh, and lie down on the sofa, completely stretched out. I look at the letter once more, lay it on my stomach, and close my eyes. Maybe when I wake up it will say something different.

———

The dried tears leave hard crust around my eyes. I can see nothing but black and I can finally smell my BO. I'm confused, shirtless, and reaching around for anything to throw over my body. My hand crunches a piece of paper and the crinkle noise reminds me of reality. Fuck that. I throw the letter to the ground, stumble toward the kitchen, open the fridge, and start downing a gallon of milk. When I finally come up for air, my eyes hit the stove clock, damn, it's 9pm. I slept right through the day.

The walk continues to the bathroom, where I don't even bother to flick on the lights, I'm sporting a piss belly and need some relief. It's only through that process I finally begin to gain my balance. I'm actually alive and human. I turn on the lights, look in the mirror, and hate what I see: a combination of Einstein and Frankenstein. Probably too generous. A monster, certainly. I splash some water on my face, nothing changes, so I do it again. Nothing. Again and again. Nothing. I tilt my head and ask myself, "Is this who I am?"

Suddenly, I hear a banging on the door. Not again. What this time? I think.

Pound, pound, pound.

"Christian, I know you're in there! I saw your car out in the lot," a voice yells. Pound, pound, pound.

I stumble my way over to the door, and the voice howls out again, "Christian, c'mon open up!"

Pound, pound, pound.

Now I'm close enough to recognize the voice, I peer through the peephole just to confirm it's Jack. Shit, what am I going to tell him?

I open the door and Jack looks me up and down. "You look like shit, dude," he says. "Ugh, and you smell like shit, too."

"I'm happy to see you too. Come in."

"I've been hitting you up all week and I've heard nothing from you. Then today I talked to Emma and I heard some shit. I didn't even know whether it was true or not. I had to come over here to see what the hell was going on. Did you quit your job!?"

I run my hand through my hair and take a deep breath.

"Something like that," I say. "It's complicated, ya know."

Jack takes a seat on the stool in the kitchen. "It doesn't sound complicated to me," he says. "It sounds like you quit your job."

"Did Emma tell you that Tim found out about everything?" I say. "That he cornered me and gave me an ultimatum?"

Jack walks over to the fridge, looks in, then responds, "What? What ultimatum? Dude, you need some fuckin' food in here. You're going to starve to death."

I proceed to tell him the abbreviated version of the story while he rummages through nothing. He snaps his head out of the fridge and stares at me.

"Wait—so you left your job for Liv?" he says. "Dude, Emma told me Liv and Tim are working on their marriage."

I sigh, pause, then yell, "Well I know that now! You gotta understand, the last time we spoke she told me she wanted to be together, in Golden Beach. Then it all happened so quickly, I had no choice. What was I supposed to do?"

"Well, for starters, not quit your fuckin' job."

This is the problem with matters of love. Nobody, not even the people closest to you, understands the nuance of the situation. They try, but everything from the outside always leans more to rational thinking, nobody can understand the emotional element to the degree it actually exists or needs to be understood. It's the most annoying thing in the world. I mean, you can't blame them, it's a near impossible task, but that's why I'm not even going to bother explaining it further to Jack. I'd rather just take the verbal beating.

"So, you've just been holed up in this place all week?" he continues. "No wonder you look and smell like ass!"

"Thanks, man."

"Sorry dude, but it's true," he says. "I won't keep breaking your balls about it. This is brutal. Have you started looking for another job?"

I look at him.

"Okay, bad question. Clearly you haven't. Well, you'll find one. You're a stud, dude. What I need you to do right now, though, is get your ass showered. We gotta get you out of this house, and go have some fun. And we're not going to talk about Liv or any of this bullshit. Got it?"

Every ounce of me wants to wallow, but Jack is probably right. Getting out is probably good, and hearing other voices beside the one in my head might be a good thing, too.

"Okay, I guess," I say. "I am fucking starving. I've been eating peanut butter and jelly all week."

Jack laughs. "You're a mess," he says. "We'll go into the city, grab a late dinner, and take it from there. Now go shower."

"Okay, give me 30 minutes to get my shit together!"

"I'm going to wait downstairs in the car, this place smells horrible. Get a house cleaner or something."

With my forehead leaning on the shower wall in front of me, the steaming hot water beats on the back of my head, and I watch it run off my body and down the drain. The filth and debris of physical and emotional wreckage is rinsing off me. Or, at least, that's the story I'm selling myself.

A night out in the city might be just what I need. Besides, I'm kind of missing my old friend Tom.

TWENTY-ONE

WAKING UP NAKED on Saturday morning in a bed you've never been in before is both exciting and scary at the same time. The story is probably good, but there's always a handful of mines that can detonate and blow your whole life up. Did I make a baby last night? Get an STD? Is she a lunatic? Those are some of the worst.

Right now, it doesn't feel like I've slept much, and I know that feeling, it actually feels more like I've been hit by a dump truck. Damn it, Christian.

I begin to feel a tug on the sheet down by my left foot, must be a dog or something. I feel two more tugs, so I pull back a little bit. This time, two words follow, "Daddy, Daddy."

My eyebrows perk, eyes slowly open up, and I pull the comforter over my head. Everything goes black for a moment and I shift my head back and forth, up and down. Is this real? The voice rings out again. The sheet pulling intensifies.

Just like MacGyver, I search for an escape route, but I've got nothing. I begin to poke around with my hands, land on a mini mountain of sorts, my God, it's a fake boob. A stark contrast from Liv's natural breasts. A jarring reminder of last night, and it starts to come back to me little by little—a nightclub, a woman who picked me up in some car, and the dusk-till-dawn partying.

Who knew one fake boob could provide so much insight? Maybe the second will give me the details. On that thought, I hear those two words again, coming from the foot of the bed, "Daddy, Daddy."

I nudge the woman next to me. "Wake up, wake up!"

She mumbles, "Wha'? What'd you say?"

I whisper, "There's a little girl pulling on the sheets calling me Daddy."

She rubs her eyes and says, "What?"

I say it again.

"Ayyyy," she shouts.

Her head snaps up and out of the comforter, starts yelling in Spanish, I have no clue what she's saying. Some lady in an apron runs into the room, grabs the little girl, and scurries back to wherever she came from. What the hell is going on?

I pull the comforter down, the sun seems to have extra power, I can barely open my eyes. I look over at her and get distracted for a moment. She's wearing pink panties and her shape is like an hourglass. I guess things could be worse, but I shake my head to snap back to reality.

"Uh, what the heck is going on?" I ask her.

"That's my daughter."

"Daughter?" I ask. "Why is she calling me Daddy!?"

She looks at me with sad eyes and a beaten look on her face. "Well . . . " she says. "Daddy lives here with me, *but* he's away on business right now."

"What!?" I say. "Is Daddy your husband?"

She turns red and more sheepish. "Yes," she mutters.

"I'm sorry I didn't tell you. We were just . . . I don't know. Having fun."

There's no light too bright to keep my eyes from opening wide now. My mind, not so much. I still can't recall the details of last night, honestly, she might have even told me about the kid. This is bad.

I just look ahead, and she says, "It's no big deal. He's probably doing the same thing."

I look around and notice that I'm in an apartment hanging from the Manhattan sky with a massive wrap-around balcony overlooking downtown. In a sober mind, that would have been my first indicator something was fishy. Or the many ripped and destroyed canvas paintings that are resting on the marble floor. What are those?

But when you're swept up in the energy of a night and a seductive smokejumper comes to put out your fire, serendipity takes hold, and you're not asking too many questions. Who has time to pay attention to details?

"Can I go outside for a moment?" I ask. "I need to get some fresh air."

"Of course, it's beautiful out."

I slide my jeans on, throw my tee over my head, and step out to the balcony to collect my thoughts. Figures that's what she says, "It's beautiful out." Just your average day in paradise, I don't even know her name, but I can barely think straight. I begin to have déjà vu. Another married woman? What the hell is wrong with me? At least I don't even remember what she feels or tastes like. If I don't remember it, did it really happen? I don't see a condom wrapper on the ground. Fuck. I hope it was good. I mean, she looks great. What is wrong with me?

I walk over to the other side of the balcony. I want to see if there are any more surprises waiting for me, so I peek through the window. Nobody in there, not even the maid or little girl. Just a sprawling living room with more paintings on the ground and an elevator that opens just to this apartment. What the hell? I shake my head, walk back a few feet on the balcony, and peer into the window. The woman has her head buried in her cellphone. It jogs my memory. Where's my phone?

I slide my hands in my pockets—phew—and pull it out. It's dead. Christ, I have no idea where I am. Some undisclosed location in the city. It's probably owned by some guy who can walk through the door at any moment. At which point, he might try to throw me off this balcony. I got to get the hell home or at least charge my phone. I touch my face to make sure I'm not dreaming, what the hell? Shit, my nose is bleeding.

I step back inside. "Do you have a tissue?"

She grabs a few from the nightstand next to the bed and points to the TV. "Must be from that over there," she says.

I look back with a tissue dangling from my right nostril. There's a bag of white powder. I look back at her and ask, "Cocaine?"

She shakes her head up and down. "You don't remember? Wow—you were messed up. I hope you remember me." She giggles.

"We ran into some American guy. Logan? Landon? We took Molly and you brought that back," she says, pointing again. "We were partying like rock stars."

Now it's starting to come back to me, there's no Logan or Landon, we ran into fucking Luke Handley. "What about my friend Jack?" I ask her. "Where is he?"

"He's the one who told you to go with me," she says, then starts screwing around on her cellphone again. Figures, but I don't have time to make sense of all this. I just want to go home.

"Any chance you can bring me back to Stamford?"

She picks her head up from her cellphone. "Connecticut?" she yells. "Honey, you weren't that good. I don't drive either."

I exhale. "You don't?"

"No. I have a driver. That's how we got here last night," she says. "My driver. He'll take you back."

"What about your husband?"

"Oh, don't worry," she says. "You think you're the first guy my driver's brought back here that wasn't my husband?"

She picks up the phone, speaks in Spanish, and all I can make out is "Stamford, Connecticut." At least I know she got that right. I gotta get the eff out of here.

I'm two seconds away from a panic attack and I can still feel my eyes rolling around in my head. I give her a kiss on the cheek, thank her for her hospitality, and tell her to keep the blow. It is the most gentlemanly thing I can muster, given the situation. Never even got her name, didn't care, she looks good, and that's the only memory I want to echo in my mind.

But the memory soon gets spoiled as I wait for the elevator to take me downstairs. I hear something scurrying around behind me, too big to be a mouse, sounds more like a child. I look over my right shoulder and spot a little blonde ponytail with two blueberry eyes staring at me.

I turn and pretend I didn't see her, check my nose for more blood, the elevator opens, and I step in, scarred for life.

I find myself right back where I started, slouched over on my couch. True to form, April showers are here, and I bet

Liv is watching the rainfall on this lazy Sunday morning. Possibly listening to some old tunes or thinking about life. Or maybe I'm just dealing with another bout of wishful thinking. Man, I miss her.

What happened to Saturday? I don't know. It's not even a memory, it's completely missing, I had to sleep all day just to get back to baseline. Some people might say Friday night is exactly what I needed. Drinking, partying, and, apparently, sex, but I feel worse. Just another bad decision in a series of many lately, only to be exacerbated by the last text I read from Jack, "Great night, wasn't it?"

But I guess I'm not some people. Friday night didn't stop my leaky heart or mend my broken career. I slept with another married woman on the "outs" and now each time I flush the toilet I can see my life spinning down the bowl. It all felt good in the moment, but it left me unsatisfied and, worse, a little girl is ruined forever.

And that's the thing I just can't shake. She's stuck in my mind like gum on a shoe. Even after you scrape it, small remnants linger, just hoping the rain will wash it away, but knowing the cold, hard ground will only embed it. It could have been Liv's daughter, my future daughter, or anyone's daughter.

I violated a principle I live by: you can do bad shit to yourself, but don't do bad shit to other people. Sure, I've danced with the underworld, but those are adults. They know what they're doing. She was a helpless child.

I have to clean my shit up.

With the apartment still a disaster, Jack was right about something, maybe I should get a house cleaner. But this seems like a good place to start for me. I begin with the bedroom, tidy up a bit, then spray down the bathroom and throw some laundry in. A smell of freshness is permeating the air, and it does make me feel a little better.

When I get back to the living room, I get hit with a wave of melancholy again. Liv's crumpled-up letter is still lying on the ground, and it's radiating heat signals to pull me in. I'm afraid to get closer, but it can't lie there forever. Ugh, I have to pick it up, but I don't have to read it.

Of course, I open it. The streaky black ink is an instant reminder that pain has been here, and hurt still bubbles in my blood. A glutton for punishment, I take a deep breath and read it again.

I don't get as sad this time around. Instead, I read it three more times. One line keeps jumping out to me, "Sometimes people flash into your life like a shooting star and remind you of all the possibilities that exist." This rocks me and I fall backward, luckily the sofa is underneath me, otherwise I'd have hit the floor.

Upon landing, I feel a stab in my right butt cheek.

I pop back up, look down, and there's nothing on the couch. I rummage through the cushions, still nothing, then it dawns on me to check my back pocket. Sure enough, I feel something broken in two pieces. I don't even need to see it to know what it is, I remember wearing these shorts in Florida. I pull out two halves of a guitar pick, one with the initial T, and the other a W.

Broken like the pick, I look back at Liv's note, and read that line again. "Sometimes people flash into your life like a shooting star and remind you of all the possibilities that exist." I hold the pick in one hand, letter in the other, and they feel like the morsel of hope I've been searching for. I'm either losing my mind or finding it.

I slip, slide, and sprint across the hardwood. I barely make it to the bedroom in one piece. I throw Liv's note and Ty's pick onto my bed and rip through everything in my closet to find the suitcase I brought to Florida. I'm throwing clothes over my shoulder. Ty's letter is somewhere in here. Ah, finally, I find it and fall back on my bed to read it.

There's a line that stops me, "The dots connected along the way, as they will with you, just always gotta look at what's in front of you." This takes the wind out of me, don't all dots always connect after you live them? I picked Liv, quit my job, she picked Tim, and now I'm here, heartbroken and jobless. It dawns on me: that's exactly what Ty was trying to tell me, which is why you always gotta look at what's in front of you.

If I stayed at Perkins, then I would have eventually become Tim, in some shape or form. Is that what I would have wanted? If I spend all my time with Jack, then I will eventually end up like Jack, in some shape or form. The dots connect themselves along the way. Is that what I want?

It hits me and she pops back into my mind. Not Liv, the blonde ponytail and two blueberry eyes staring at me— the vulnerable little girl. Am I one of those dots? How will her dots connect?

Still holding the note, I finish it. "Don't kill yourself with consumption, kid," Ty wrote. "I'll never tell you anything more important than that." I put the paper down and stare at the white ceiling. I listen to the rain streaming down the window and laundry tumbling in the dryer.

Ty was on a consumption diet, something I'd never heard before, but maybe it's necessary for our consumer-driven lifestyles. Always balancing the consumption with creation. The inevitable with the avoidable. The passive with the active. Perhaps life goes down easier that way. Or at least, tastes a little better.

Have I created anything today? Seems like a daunting task. I know I didn't make a movie, paint a painting, or write a song, but is it possible that I've created *nothing*? What have I even done today? I ate some old cereal, watched TV, listened to music, and cleaned up a bit. The only thing that actually made me feel decent was cleaning the apartment. I guess I did create a clean environment. Maybe my view of creation is too small.

And then there's Liv.

With her it wasn't the things that brought me close to her, it was the relationship and experiences we created together. And now she lives inside me forever. "Never lose that playfulness," was the last thing she wrote me. "Life is too hard."

As the rain continues to run on the window, I lift my head up and look around. I see Ty's broken guitar pick, and, rather than piece it together, I pick up my own. I grab a pad and pen, jot down some lines, and strum a few chords.

I take solace knowing that my next Tom Collins might be the best I ever had.

ACKNOWLEDGMENTS

I am extremely grateful to everyone who helped in the creation of this novel.

To my editing team—Chantel Hamilton, Stacey Covell, and Kirstyn Smith. Without your expertise, taste, and fine eyes, this book would only be a fraction of what it turned out to be.

To my folks—Don and Donna Vigliotti, you've endured many of my Sunday dinner rants. In the many shapes and turns of my life, your support has been nothing short of amazing.

To my oldest brother and sister-in-law—Darron and Geralyn Vigliotti, as terrifying as the first draft is for a writer, braving it as a reader is the ultimate show of support.

To my podcast team—Dave Lishansky, producer-extra-ordinaire; and Adam Cunliffe, voice-actor-extraordinaire, you are both true craftsmen. Who knew Christian Ballantine could sound this good?

To my friends—Many of you have spent late nights at my place listening to me read excerpts from *Tom Collins*.

Pretty sure you laugh about it the next day, but that's okay. You're all a bunch of assholes, anyway. Love you, guys.

To my readers—Without you, this whole thing would be pointless. Well, maybe not pointless. But you get the idea. Writing to no one sucks. I'm so honored to entertain you. Please, please keep reading. I need you.

To my heroes—All the writers, musicians, and film-makers who serve as my teachers and inspiration. Although many of you will never read these sentences, this is an opportunity to highlight the true power of creative work. It has the ability to transcend time and space. Quite simply, *Tom Collins* would not exist without you.

To anyone I missed—It was not intentional. I appreciate you, I promise.

Thank you!

ABOUT THE AUTHOR

DOUGLAS VIGLIOTTI is a writer and storyteller who believes less is more and intention is everything. He has authored multiple nonfiction books, (most notably) *The Gap*, way too many articles, and one ebook, *Pumpernickel & Peanut Butter: Why Weird Works,* which is free at DouglasVigliotti.com. *Tom Collins* is his first work of fiction. You can listen to the novel on *Slightly Crooked: Good Stories, Told Well,* a first-of-its-kind podcast that features the audiobooks of his novels. He lives in New Haven, CT.

facebook.com/slightlycrooked

instagram.com/douglasvigliotti

ONE LAST THING

If you're interested in any future novels I write, please click here to join my mailing list: **newbooks. douglasvigliotti.com**. (Yup, there are more novels on the way.)

I'll email you when I have a new book available, and, as a thank you for joining, you'll receive exclusive offers (discounts, giveaways, etc.) for each new release, as well as a complimentary copy of my ebook, *Pumpernickel & Peanut Butter: Why Weird Works*.

Thanks again for reading *Tom Collins*. Your readership and support mean the world to me.

DOUGLAS VIGLIOTTI, 2021

Made in United States
North Haven, CT
18 November 2021

11275807R00133